我的第一本
經典故事
親子英文

My First Family English
of Classic Stories

9789864541362.zip

iOS系統請升級至iOS 13後再行下載，此為大型檔案，建議使用WIFI
連線下載，以免佔用流量，並確認連線狀況，以利下載順暢。

　　各位爸爸、媽媽，各位小朋友們，大家好。我是外語啟蒙教學發展學會的李宗玥老師。在從事兒童美語教學這數十年以來，發現很多家長都有這樣的盲點：明明花了很多錢，買了昂貴的英語教材，卻又礙於時間及能力等問題，無法好好地運用這些教材與孩子互動，甚至不久就只是擺在書架上，或放在角落積灰塵。

　　沒錯，真正的關鍵，不是在書是純原文、國外進口、價格昂貴上，而是在能不能好好的運用教材跟孩子互動，引發孩子學習英文的興趣！所以，在數年前我出版了《我的第一本親子英文》，幫助了許多家庭打造了英語學習環境後，我們在此全新推出一本很有趣、針對「親子英文閱讀」的英文學習書籍 ──《我的第一本經典故事親子英文》。這本親子閱讀書籍中的故事內容，都是來自最受歡迎的童話或寓言故事，由此來導入英文學習，相信每位家長都能輕鬆使用，不但可以培養親子感情，更可以教孩子一些人生的價值觀，可謂一舉兩得。

　　書中逗趣的插圖仍延伸自《我的第一本親子英文》的Peter家族，相信廣大讀者對於這些人物應該是記憶猶新。此外，在您與孩子一起閱讀的時候，適時指出對應的單字圖片，讓他們在剛開始接觸英文時，就能懂意思，可增加他們學習的成就感與興趣。而且，本書提供的MP3光碟，從中英對照的錄音中，小朋友可自然而然融入這個故事的世界裡面。藉此，父母們可以自然地培養出孩子對英文的理解力，並藉此建立他的國際觀與價值觀，引導他們思考人生的方向和意義。如此才不會投入了大筆的教育經費，最後卻養出一個只會應付考試，不

知未來為何，也無法善用英文知識，為自己人生帶來更多利益和機會的人。

　　本書以中英文對照，改編 15 則世界經典故事，並加上導讀問答、英文字彙、片語、相關句型、文法的說明，以及與故事內容相關的知識補給站，這些設計都讓家長能夠更簡單的運用本書與小朋友們互動。當然，英語老師使用這本書，也可以很輕易的掌握學生的學習效果及進度。此外，我們每一篇故事都不是死板板、照本宣科的把原來的故事搬到書中而已，而是做了一些有趣的改編，例如在《虛榮的烏鴉》（Cody the Little Crow）這一則故事中，我們顛覆了原本那隻「虛榮」（vanity）的烏鴉所扮演的負面角色，而以「為了給媽媽買最棒的生日禮物而口袋空空」的烏鴉取代之，而最後，每一篇故事的結局，都會留下一個意想不到，且耐人尋味的思考空間，讓孩子們更能將故事烙印在腦海裡。

　　本書雖然是以親子共讀為出發點，但所提出的理念、方向及建議，是對於全天下的父母們，對於孩子的英語教育一個「遠見」的觀念。其實，不論是哪個學科，孩子若能透過家長一開始正確的理念及方法，獲得共學及美好的生活經驗中的養分，便能自然而然地自發性學習。這是一本相當值得推薦給家長、學生、老師們的初學英文閱讀教材。

本書使用說明

從小培養孩子在閱讀童話故事中記單字，自然而然接受英文！

　　孩子的英文學習過程，如同一趟發現孩子天賦的旅途。本書的單元設計，可以幫助您引導孩子們選擇自己想要的英文學習之旅，讓他們在這趟旅途中，來腳步輕盈、輕鬆又自在，並感受到學習英文的無上樂趣。

單元主題
每一單元首頁都有兩張詮釋單元主題的卡通圖片，不但幫助學習，同時也激發想像力。

中、英文並重，培養雙語優勢
每一篇故事都有整齊對應的中英文內容，家長們都能輕鬆使用，不會礙於自身英文程度的問題而望文興嘆！

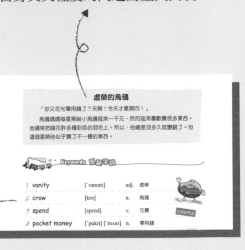

QR碼線上音檔
手機隨時一掃，任何地方都能共享受親子學習樂趣

關鍵字詞
每個單元分成三個段落，每個段落都有課文中出現的關鍵字詞（單字+片語）解釋。

輕鬆問答

每個段落結束後，會有一個雙向
互動的腦激盪問題，家長也可以
藉此和孩子一起討論喔！

feathers. So, he always becomes poor **before long**.
有一句話說 "Birds of a feather flock together." 就是「物以類聚」的意思。
But this week, **it seems he bought** something
也可以寫成 he seemed to have bought
different.

Pause & Answer 動動腦

1. How often does Cody get his pocket money?
（寇弟多久拿一次零用錢？）

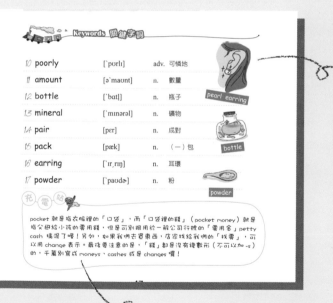

Keywords 關鍵字詞

10	**poorly**	[ˈpʊrlɪ]	adv.	可憐地
11	**amount**	[əˈmaʊnt]	n.	數量
12	**bottle**	[ˈbatl]	n.	瓶子
13	**mineral**	[ˈmɪnərəl]	n.	礦物
14	**pair**	[per]	n.	成對
15	**pack**	[pæk]	n.	（一）包
16	**earring**	[ˈɪrˌrɪŋ]	n.	耳環
17	**powder**	[ˈpaʊdə]	n.	粉

pearl earring

bottle

powder

充電站

pocket 就是指衣服裡的「口袋」，而「口袋裡的錢」（pocket money）就是
指父母給小孩的零用錢。但是可別跟用於一般公司行號的「零用金」petty
cash 搞混了喔！另外，如果我們去買東西，店家找給我們的「找零」，可
以用 change 表示。最後要注意的是，「錢」卻是沒有複數形（不可以加 -s）
的，千萬別寫成 moneys、cashes 或是 changes 喔！

圖像記憶

每個段落的鍵字詞
中，會再精選出幾
個字詞，搭配逗趣
可愛的圖案來呈
現，達到更佳的記
憶效果！

充電站

針對這個段落中出現的特殊字詞
或觀念，補充您意想不到、容易
用錯的表達用語。

精選句型與解析

每個段落中以粉色標示之句型，將於後面「精選句型」中進一步解說。

Useful Expressions 精選句型

spend money / time on… 把錢／時間花在…

→ You need to spend more time on your schoolwork.
你得花更多時間在學校功課上。

主詞 + give + 物 + to + 人 給某人某物

→ My daddy gave a present to mom.
= My daddy gave mom a present.
我爸給了媽媽一個禮物。

make a plan to + V 計畫去做…

→ Let's make a plan to buy mom a surprise gift.
我們來計畫給媽媽買一份驚喜的禮物。

Sentence Patterns 句型解析

◆ 無論是「花時間」或是「花錢」都可以用這個動詞喔！比如說：
I spent NT$50 on this book.（我花了 50 元買這本書。）
My teacher spent the time after school teaching me English.
（我的老師在放學後還花時間教我英文。）

◆ give 這個動詞有點特別，因為它後面可以有兩個受詞，我們把它稱作「授予動詞」：
I gave the lucky cake to my mom.（我把這幸運蛋糕給了媽媽。）
= I gave my mom the lucky cake.
→ "my mom" 和 "the lucky cake" 都是 gave 的受詞喔！

◆ 雖然有時候計畫趕不上變化，但是我們做事情還是得「有所計畫」（make a plan）才好。那麼，「計畫要做某事」就可以這麼說：
You need to make a plan to study English.（你得開始計畫念英文了。）
= You need to plan to study English.

我們出去玩囉！
YA!
Don't you make a plan?

Mama Crow gives Cody the little crow 1000 dollars once a week. But Cody likes to buy a lot of things. He usually spends his money on many kinds of colorful feathers. So, he always becomes poor before long. But this week, it seems he bought something different.

是「一次」的意思，「兩次」就是 twice。

有一句話說 "Birds of a feather flock together."，就是「物以類聚」的意思。

也可以寫成 he seemed to have bought

片語解析

before long

◆ 什麼叫作「在長長久久之前」啊？
大家都知道 before 是「在…之前」的意思，所以像 before dark（在天黑以前）、before day（在天亮之前）都是很好理解的片語，不過，before long 這個片語，正確理解它的意思是「在時間拉長以前」，就是「不會過太久」的意思囉！

 Wow! They are dating! I think they must fall in love before long!
哇噢！他們在約會耶！我想他們很快就會陷入熱戀了！

I hope to get home before dark.
（我希望在天黑之前回到家。）

片語解析

以粗體標示的片語，會在每個單元的「片語解析」中講解，及其衍生用法。

文法解析

文法雖然是是學習英文的過程中
比較嚴肅且枯燥的部分，但本書
搭配生動有趣的漫畫插圖，加上
平易近人的文字講解，相信家長
與孩子都可以很快地吸收喔！

 與「上廁所」有關的英文

廁所裡面這些東西的英文怎麼說，你都會了嗎？

(1) air freshener 空氣芳香劑	(2) towel rack 毛巾架	(3) mirror 鏡子
(4) tissue 面紙	(5) toilet paper 衛生紙	(6) soap dispenser 給皂器
(7) hand dryer 烘手機	(8) urinal 小便斗	(9) toilet 馬桶
(10) plunger 馬桶吸盤	(11) washbowl 洗臉盆	(12) toilet brush 馬桶刷

文法解析 動詞的現在簡單式

第一、用來表示「狀態」或「事實」，比如說：

Hardy and Ethan are good friends.
（哈弟和伊森是好朋友。）
→ 表示他們是好朋友的狀態

She is a teacher.（她是一位老師。）
→ be 動詞 is 表示一種事實

第二、表示習慣或重複性的行為

常與every day、often、always、usually、
sometimes……等「頻率副詞」一起使用。

They always go to the bathroom after waking up.
（他們總是在起床後去上廁所。）
→ 表示他們每天早上的習慣。這應該也是很多人
的習慣吧！所以要用現在簡單式來表示。

Hardy sometimes has bowel movements after breakfast.
（哈弟有時候會在早餐過後上大號。）
→ 表示一種「偶爾」的生活習慣，也許是一個星期一次或兩次。

字詞一籮筐

透過有趣又好記的圖案，幫助家
長與孩子「一口氣地」學會「各
種餐點」、「十二生肖」、
「十二個月份」、「居家環境各
個設施」……的英文大集合。

人物介紹

DAD 爸爸

36 歲，在貿易公司上班，喜歡假日時帶著孩子們一起去戶外運動，十分關心孩子的學習狀況，喜歡看棒球、看電視、種植花草。

MOM 媽媽

33 歲，家庭主婦，擅長料理，最拿手的一道菜是咖哩飯；把家裡打掃得很乾淨，看到小朋友把家裡弄得亂七八糟的時候，會大聲罵人喔！

PETER 弟弟

7 歲，國小二年級，喜歡吃甜食、打電動，愛賴床，常常和媽媽撒嬌。跟姊姊 Jenny 平常感情還不錯，但偶而還是會吵架。心情好的時候會幫忙做些家事，最要好的朋友是 Andy。

JENNY 姊姊

9 歲，國小四年級，興趣是看書和彈鋼琴，
比較黏爸爸。喜歡上學，但不喜歡補習，數
學不太好，但英文還不錯。

ANDY 同學

7 歲，Peter 的同班同學也是他最要好的朋友，
很有禮貌的小男孩，喜歡打籃球。

馬鈴薯

隨時可能會出現的萬能串場人物，會以各種
不同顏色、形狀、以及角色出現。

Contents

Contents

Contents

Unit 1
聞雞起舞

精選句型　❶ It's time to + V

❷ Don't be so...

❸ You'd better... or...

片語解析　Wear / Put on a long face

文法解析　名詞單複數

Don't waste time watching TV, OK?

MP3 ★ Track1

Cock-a-doodle-doo...
get up!

"Cock-a-doodle-doo, get up, it's time to

study again!"

Mr. Cock wakes up Zu-Ti every morning because

wake up 也可以等於 waken 或 awaken 喔！

he promises to study three hours before school. Mr.

promise + to-V 表示「答應要去做⋯」。

Cock is just like his alarm clock. But this morning, Zu-

這個字也有「警報器」的意思喔！

Ti was being a little lazy, and he overslept. "Zu-Ti, it's

oversleep 的過去式。

time to get up!" Mr. Cock yelled angrily.

Pause & Answer 動動腦

1. How long does Zu-Ti study before school?

（祖逖上學前要念多久的書？）

解答在 P.224

聞雞起舞！

　　「咕咕咕，起床啦，讀書的時間又到了！」公雞先生每天早上叫祖迷起床，因為祖迷希望可以在上學前先讀三個小時的書，而公雞先生就像是他的鬧鐘一樣。不過，這一天早上，祖迷有點偷懶而睡過頭。所以公雞先生生氣地大喊：「祖迷！該起床啦！」

Keywords 關鍵字詞

1	wake up	['wek ˌʌp]	v.	叫…起床
2	promise	['prɑmɪs]	v.	答應，允諾
3	before school		adv.	上學前
4	alarm clock	[əˈlɑrm ˈklɑk]	n.	鬧鐘
5	lazy	['lezɪ]	adj.	懶惰的
6	oversleep	['ovɚ'slip]	v.	睡過頭
7	yell	[jɛl]	v.	喊叫
8	angrily	['æŋgrɪlɪ]	adv.	生氣地

wake up

alarm clock

angrily

cock-a-doodle-doo 公雞叫聲
（一般出現在童謠或詩集中，可別以為是 ku-ku-ku 喔！）
在英文裡，我們常用 crow 來表示「公雞的啼叫聲」，而母雞的「咯咯聲」是 chuck。另外，母雞在下蛋之後，還會發出一種叫聲，叫作 cackle。最後，鴨子的叫聲，一般用 quack 表示。

"Ten more minutes, please!" Zu-Ti **wore a long face**

「再十分鐘」可別說成 "More ten minutes." 喔！

and answered slowly.

"Ten more minutes? What time is it now? It's already six

o'clock! Don't be so lazy. Hurry up! You have to get up

也等於 Quickly 這個字。

and study." Mr. Cock strengthened his voice.

從名詞 strength（力氣）衍生而來的。

"Everything is excellent in the morning. Don't waste

稱讚別人時，也可以用這個字喔！

time! Cock-a-doodle-doo, get up at once!" Mr. Cock

也等於 right away 或
right now。

continued.

"Alright, alright, I'll get up…" Zu-Ti answered lazily.

也可以說 All right!

Pause & Answer 動動腦

2. How did Zu-Ti answer Mr. cock?

（祖狄如何回答公雞先生呢？）

解答在 P.224

祖逖擺出一副臭臉且緩慢地回答：「再十分鐘，拜託！」公雞先生提高聲調說：「再十分鐘？你以為現在幾點？已經六點啦！別這麼懶了，動作快！快起床讀書。」公雞先生繼續說，「早晨的一切是美好的，別再浪費時間了，咕咕咕，馬上起床！」

　　「好啦，好啦，我要起床了……」祖逖懶洋洋地回答。

Keywords 關鍵字詞

9	wear a long face		ph.	擺臭臉
10	hurry up	['hɜɪ,ʌp]	v.	（使）快一點
11	strengthen	['strɛŋθən]	v.	加強
12	voice	[vɔɪs]	n.	聲音
13	excellent	['ɛks!ənt]	adj.	極棒的
14	waste time		ph.	浪費時間
15	at once	[æt] [wʌns]	adv.	立刻
16	continue	[kən'tɪnjʊ]	v.	繼續
17	alright	['ɔl'raɪt]	adv.	好吧

hurry up

excellent

 充 電 站

Everything is excellent in the morning! 早晨的一切都是美好的！在英文裡，與「早起」有關的諺語還有「一日之計在於晨」、「早起的鳥兒有蟲吃」。這兩句話的英文分別是 An hour in the morning is worth two in the evening. 以及 The early bird catches the worm. ，同學們，記住了嗎？

He yawned and stretched a little bit. Then he rose

「打哈欠」+「伸懶腰」，兩個字要一起記下來喲！

to brush his teeth, wash his face, and study his

單數是 tooth

schoolwork.

"Very well! I hope you can keep this good habit" Mr.

Cock encourages him.

en（形成動詞）+ courage（勇氣）→ 給予勇氣，就是「鼓勵」的意思囉！

"But you'd better change your clothes, or you will be

late for school!"

Pause & Answer 動動腦

3. What did Zu-Ti do after getting up?

（祖狄起床後做了哪些事？）

解答在 P.224

他打了個呵欠，伸了個懶腰，然後去刷牙洗臉，接著溫習功課。

公雞先生鼓勵祖逖說：「非常好！我希望你能保持這個好習慣。「不過你現在最好去換衣服，不然你上學要遲到了喔！」

Keywords 關鍵字詞

18	yawn	[jɔn]	v.	打哈欠
19	stretch	[strɛtʃ]	v.	伸懶腰
20	rise	[raɪz]	v.	起床（過去式為 rose）
21	brush one's teeth			刷牙
22	schoolwork	['skul͵wɝk]	n.	學校功課
23	keep this good habit			保持這樣的好習慣
24	encourage	[ɪn'kɝɪdʒ]	v.	鼓勵
25	be late for school			上學遲到

brush one's teeth

yawn

encourage

充電站

日常生活中，我們常常會有「遲到」的情形，我們常常會說 "I'm sorry for being late."（抱歉我遲到了。）或是 "I'm sorry to keep you waiting.l"（抱歉讓你久等了。）如果要「再抱歉一點」，可以說 "Sorry, I'm late again. I'll make it up to you. Dinner is on me."（抱歉我又遲到了。我會補償你的。晚餐我請客）而爸爸媽媽們平成上班或社交時，也常會說到 "Sorry, I was delayed by a last-minute meeting."（抱歉，我因為臨時開會所以遲到了。）

Useful Expressions 精選句型

It's time to + V 該是去做…的時候了

→ It's (almost) time (for you) to go to bed.
（你）該上床睡覺了。

Don't be so… 別這麼…

→ Don't be so sad/proud/angry.
別這麼傷心 / 臭屁 / 生氣！

You'd better… or… 你最好…，不然……

→ You'd better study harder, or (else) you won't pass the test.
你最好用功點，不然你無法通過考試。

● "It's time to get up!" 「該起床了！」，還記得公雞先生見到祖逖賴床時所說的這句話嗎？這個句型的意思正是「該是……的時候了」。我們可以套用在許多地方，唯一須注意的是：to 後面要接「原形動詞」，for 後面接「名詞」。So now, it's time to practice the sentence pattern!（所以現在，是來練習這個句型的時候了！）

It's time to do my homework. 該寫作業了。
It's time for my homework.

● You'd 是 You had 的縮寫。had better 是一個助動詞，後面要接原形動詞，也可以寫成 had best 或 may as well，用來表示「建議」某人去做某事，可搭配連接詞 or（否則）來表示，如果沒去做會有什麼不好的下場。

● 那麼，大家來練習一下這一句要怎麼寫囉：

「該上床睡覺了。你最好是早睡早起，否則明天又要遲到了。」

_____

_____

解答在 P.224

wear / put on a long face
（擺臭臉）

● 「穿上一張長長的臉」？這什麼意思啊？

在解釋之前，先請大家做一個動作：用手把自己的臉盡可能地拉長，然後去照照鏡子，或許就能知道 wear a long face 是什麼意思了。我們的表情看起來應該是一臉不開心吧？（萬一是開心的話，可能要去醫院檢查了），看起來是不是「**愁眉苦臉**」的樣子？好像故事裡的祖逖剛起床的模樣。由此可知，wear 除了有我們平常所熟知的「穿戴」的意思，還能指人臉上所「顯露」出來的表情。 當然，wear 可以用 put on 來取代喔！比如說：

She always wears a long face.
她總是愁眉苦臉。

She always wears a smile on her face
她總是笑容可掬。

He was putting on a long face when he got up.
他起床的時候一臉不爽的樣子。

24

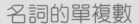

名詞的單複數

話說公雞先生剛開始叫他們起床的時候，也是慢條斯理。所以第一天祖逖只讀了**一個小時**（one hour），又去睡回籠覺。過了一星期，時間增加到**兩個小時**（two hours），過了兩星期，好不容易增加到**三個小時**（three hours）。

咦？聰明的讀者有沒有注意到英文的部分出現什麼變化？（趕快再看一遍）沒錯！祖逖讀書的時間從 one hour 變成 two hours 又變成 three hours。知道這是什麼規則嗎？

這一點是英文和中文在處理名詞單複數時十分不一樣的地方。中文無論數量多寡，從 1 到 99999 都不會影響名詞。但英文除了單數之外，「幾乎」（凡事必有例外）都要在字尾做一些改變。就讓 RK 老師用底下簡單的表格來解釋這個概念吧！

中文	一個小時	兩個小時	三個小時	九萬九千九百九十九個小時
English	1 hour	2 hours	3 hours	99999 hours（也讀太久了……）

很乾淨，沒有跟屁蟲

多了個 s

雖然數目變很大，但還是只有多一個 s

由此可知，英文名詞在單數以外的狀況下，需要在字尾加 s，「**那名詞後面原本就有 s 的要怎麼辦？也是再加一個 s 嗎？**」，老師就知道我們好學的讀者一定會提出這樣的問題，別擔心，老師早已經準備好另一個表格來回答這個問題。

字尾是……	怎麼辦？	舉例
大部分的名詞	+ s	star → stars
「母音 + y」	+ s	day → days
-s -x -sh -ch	+ es	box → boxes
「子音 + o」		hero → heroes
「子音 + y」	去 y 加 ies	enemy → enemies
-f 或 -fe	去 f/fe 加 ves	life → lives

此外，有些名詞的複數變化並不是加 s，也就是所謂的不規則變化，這邊也特地整理出一些常見的例子給大家參考，避免使用錯誤。

男人	man	→	men	女人	woman	→	women
小孩	child	→	children	腳	foot	→	feet
老鼠	mouse	→	mice	牙齒	tooth	→	teeth
魚	fish	→	fish	綿羊	sheep	→	sheep

與「睡覺」有關的英文

　　以下是我們每天都用得到的，且發生在我們周遭的日常生活睡覺大小事，趕快來學學這些最道地的表達用語吧！

(1) sleepy	想睡覺	(1) drowsy	昏昏欲睡
(2) sweet dreams	一夜好眠	(3) take a nap	小睡片刻
(4) catch up on sleep	補眠	(1) doze off	打瞌睡
(5) snore	打呼	(6) toss and turn	輾轉難眠
sleep like a log	睡死了	night owl	夜貓子

親子英文共讀筆記欄

可以把不熟悉的
單字片語寫在這邊喔！

Unit 2
老鼠與鈴鐺貓

精選句型	主詞 + be coming soon
	身體部位 + be + (still) killing me
	人 + feel much better (now)
片語解析	Hang On
文法解析	動詞現在簡單式

MP3★Track2

The Mice and the Belled Cat

Hardy and Ethan are good friends.

They always go to the bathroom after

bathroom（浴室，洗手間）和bedroom（臥室）可別搞混了喲！

waking up. But, they have to be

和 must（必須）的意思很接近

careful. As long as they heard the bell ring, it means

hear 的過去式（不規則變化）

the cat, Bossy, is coming soon. They usually run away

before the cat comes. But this time, Ethan had a

bad stomach.

bad stomach 就是「吃壞肚子」的意思！

"Oh, no! My stomach is still killing me," Ethan said.

不是真的「殺」，是「很痛」的意思

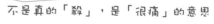

Pause & Answer 動動腦

1. What happened to Ethan when the cat was coming?
   (當那隻貓要來了的時候，伊森怎麼了？)

解答在 P.224

老鼠與鈴鐺貓

哈弟和伊森是非常要好的朋友。他們起床要做的第一件事情就是上廁所。但他們必須小心翼翼，只要聽到鈴噹的聲音，就代表貓咪伯西來了。他們通常在這隻貓來到前就逃走。可是這一次伊森卻肚子痛。

伊森說：「噢，不行！我的肚子還是痛得不得了！」

Keywords 關鍵字詞

1	careful	[`kɛrfəl]	adj.	小心翼翼的
2	as long as		conj.	只要
3	ring	[rɪŋ]	v.	（鈴聲）響起
4	bell	[bɛl]	v.	繫鈴
5	run away	[`rʌnə͵we]	v.	逃走
6	bad stomach	[bæd] [`stʌmək]	n.	鬧肚子
7	quickly	[`kwɪklɪ]	adv.	快點
8	coming soon	[`kʌmɪŋ] [sun]		快來了

careful

run away

bad stomach

充電站

英文裡，表示「廁所」的字好多，比如 toilet 是指一般「有馬桶的」廁所，而 bathroom 是「有浴缸的」那種廁所。另外，restroom 通常指「公共場所」或是一些大型「遊覽車、飛機上的」廁所，而 W.C. 也是經常在公共場所可以見到的，它是 water closet（沖水馬桶）的縮寫，不過它比較常用在「標示牌上」，而不是在說話的時候喔！

Ten minutes later...

這句也可以說 After ten minutes…

"Aha! I feel much better now!" Ethan said happily.

"Oh...no... I think I need to take number two," Hardy

「尿尿」是1號，那麼2號就是…懂了吧！

said.

"No problem. I'll keep a lookout for you," Ethan said.

look + out → 「看出去」，就是「把風」的意思囉！

"Gee... the toilet is way too dirty..." Hardy said.

Another five minutes later... Ethan heard the bell ring.

hear 的過去式，只要加一個 d 就可以囉！

"Speed up! Bossy is COMING!" Ethan shouted.

當名詞是「速度」的意思

Pause & Answer 動動腦

2. How long did Ethan spend in the bathroom?
   (伊森在廁所待了多久的時間？)

解答在 P.224

32

十分鐘過後……伊森愉快地說：「啊哈！總算舒服多了。」

哈弟：「哦……糟糕……換我想要上大號了。」

伊森：「沒問題！我來幫你把風。」

哈弟：「哇，這個廁所也太髒了吧！」

又過了五分鐘，伊森聽到了鈴鐺聲。

伊森大叫：「快一點！伯西要來了！」

Keywords 關鍵字詞

9	later	[ˋletɚ]	adv.	後來
10	take number two	[tek] [ˋnʌmbɚ] [tu]	v.	上大號
11	lookout	[ˋlʊkˋaʊt]	n.	警戒，監視
12	toilet	[ˋtɔɪlɪt]	n.	廁所
13	way too	[we] [tu]	adv.	非常地
14	another	[əˋnʌðɚ]	adj.	另一個的
15	speed up	[ˋspidʌp]	v.	快一點
16	shout	[ʃaʊt]	v.	喊叫

lookout

toilet

speed up

「去小便」當然也可以說是 take number one！除了用 take，我們也可以用 go for 來表示。另外，我們也可以用 "I want to pee."、"I want to take a piss." 來表示「我要去尿尿。」以及 "I want to poo." 來表示「我要上大號。」還有，shit 這個字除了拿來罵人，也可以表示「大便」。很多老外都會直接說 I wanna shit now！（我現在想去大便）。

"The toilet is plugged up!" Hardy cried.

記得被動式加 -ed 之前要重複 g 喔！

"Forget it! Let's get out of here now..." Ethan said.

「忘記它」就是「算了吧！」的意思

Luckily, Hardy and Ethan ran away right before the cat showed up.

"Hardy... Ethan... anybody there?" Bossy said.

這是 Is anybody there? 的省略說法

"Yes... Boss... what can we do for you?" Ethan and Hardy answered.

"There is no tissue paper in the bathroom..." Bossy said.

tissue paper 可不等於 paper tissues（紙巾）喔！

"Hang on there, Boss... I'm coming!" Hardy said with tissue and mustard...

介系詞 with 表示「帶著…」

Pause & Answer 動動腦

3. What did the cat ask for?

（這隻貓要求了什麼？）

解答在 P.224

哈弟叫喊著：「馬桶堵住了啦！」

伊森說：「算了啦！我們趕快閃……」

幸運地，他們剛好在伯西出現之前就逃走了。

伯西：「哈弟……伊森……有人在嗎？」

伊森、哈弟回答：「是的……老大，有什麼可以效勞的嗎？」

伯西：「廁所裡沒衛生紙了……」

哈弟：「老大撐著點，我來了！」手上還拿著衛生紙和芥末……

Keywords 關鍵字詞

17	plug up	[`plʌg͵ʌp]	v.	堵塞；塞住
18	forget	[fɚ`gɛt]	v.	忘記
19	show up	[`ʃo͵ʌp]	v.	出現
20	right before…	[raɪt] [bɪ`for]	conj	就在…之前
21	tissue paper	[`tɪʃʊ] [`pepɚ]	n.	衛生紙
22	hang on	[hæŋ] [an]	v.	等一下
23	mustard	[`mʌstɚd]	n.	芥末

plugged up

forget

充電站

plug 本來是指用來堵住排水口的「塞子」，當動詞用就是「把…塞住」的意思。另外，我們家裡電器用品的「插頭」也叫 plug，比如說：put the plug into the socket（將插頭插進插座中）。那如果是「拔掉插頭」或「把塞子拔掉」，可以說 unplug。比如：unplug the electric pot（把電鍋插頭拔掉）。

Useful Expressions 精選句型

主詞 + be coming soon …快要來了

→ A strong typhoon is coming soon!
　強颱快來囉！

身體部位 + be + (still) killing me 我的…（還是）好痛

→ My back is still killing me. I'm not moving well now.
　我的背還是好痛。我現在沒辦法好好移動。

人 + feel much better (now) 某人（現在）感覺好多了

→ I'm feeling much better now. Just don't worry.
　我現在感覺好多了。就別擔心了。

36

Sentence Patterns 句型解析

- 相信大家平常在電視或廣播節目的尾聲,都會看到或聽到 Coming soon! 的字眼。另外,像是爸媽叫我們時,也可以回答說:I'm coming!。或者有人問誰怎麼還沒到時,也可回答說:He is coming soon!。或者小朋友最喜歡的「過年」快到時,也可以說 "The New Year's coming (soon)." 不過,可別說成 The New Year's coming quickly / fast!(✕)喔!

- 表達身體某個部位「很痛」,用 kill 真是最恰當不過了!另外,表示「病痛」、「一段不堪為首的往事」、「很差的成績」…等,也可以用 kill。比如說:The bad grade is really killing me!(這爛成績讓我非常非常難過啊!)

- 到醫院探望親友時,最常問的一句話就是 "How do you feel now?" 或者說 "Do you feel any better?" 這時候可以回答 "I feel much better now." 或 是 "I feel a lot better now."。

hang on

● 這是「掛著」、「掛上去」，還是「掛了」的意思呢？

hang 本身有「懸掛」的意思，東西掛在牆上，除非有人去移動，不然都是固定在那邊一動也不動的，而介系詞 on 本身就有「持續」的意思，比如說 go on、keep on，或是電源開關切到 ON 的位置，表示一個「開啟的狀態」。所以說，hang on 也有「停留」的意思。而 just a second 也和這裡的 hang on 有異曲同工之妙，其他像是 hold on、just a moment 也都有相同意思喔。比如說：

The picture is hanging on the wall.
這幅畫掛在牆上。

**Please hang on there.
I'll be back soon.**
請在這那裏等一下。我很快回來。

Don't let unhappy things hang on your mind.
別一直牽掛著不愉快的事。

動詞的現在簡單式

呵呵，小朋友們別看到「文法」這兩個字就飛奔逃離了！其實現在式簡單式真的很「簡單」，以最簡單的方式來説，只要看到主詞加上原形動詞就是現在簡單式。

當然，現在簡單式的一個比較「不簡單」的地方，就是「單數」動詞的規則與不規則變化，這跟第一單元的名詞單複數變化其實有點像喔！

<table>
<tr><th colspan="2">規則</th><th>範例</th></tr>
<tr><td rowspan="3">規則
變化</td><td>在動詞的字尾加-s</td><td>cook → cooks、take → takes
drink → drinks、eat → eats</td></tr>
<tr><td>動詞的字尾若為-ch、-s、-x、
-sh或-o時，字尾加-es。</td><td>teach → teaches、fix → fixes
kiss → kisses、go → goes</td></tr>
<tr><td>動詞的字尾若為「子音 + -y」，
則去-y，並在字尾加-ies；字尾
若為「母音 + -y」，則直接加
上 –s即可，。</td><td>fly → flies 、cry → cries
buy → buys、play → plays
say → says</td></tr>
<tr><td colspan="2">不規則
變化</td><td>have → has、are → is、do → does</td></tr>
</table>

再來，我們也要知道「現在簡單式」的使用情形：

第一、用來表示「狀態」或「事實」，比如說：

Hardy and Ethan are good friends.
（哈弟和伊森是好朋友。）
→ 表示他們是好朋友的狀態

She is a teacher.（她是一位老師。）
→ be 動詞 is 表示一種事實

第二、表示習慣或重覆性的行為

常與every day、often、always、usually、
sometimes……等「頻率副詞」一起使用。

是從after they wake up簡化而來的

They always go to the bathroom after waking up.
（他們總是在起床後去上廁所。）
→ 表示他們每天早上的習慣。這應該也是很多人
　的習慣吧！所以要用現在簡單式來表示。

bowel是「腸」的意思，而「腸道運動」（bowel
movement）就是指文中「二號」（number two）。

Hardy sometimes has bowel movements after breakfast.
（哈弟有時候會在早餐過後上大號。）
→ 表示一種「偶爾」的生活習慣，也許是一個星期一次或兩次。

第三、表示「不變的真理」或「格言」

The sun rises from the east.（太陽從東邊升起。）
Every dog has his day.（風水輪流轉。）

太陽從東邊升起，西邊落下。這並不是昨天或今天
才剛始的事。這個狀態是從數十億年前就持續至今日，
而且往後也會一直持續下去的不變現象。

40

與「上廁所」有關的英文

廁所裡面這些東西的英文怎麼説，你都會了嗎？

(1) air freshener	空氣芳香劑	(2) towel rack	毛巾架	(3) mirror	鏡子
(4) tissue	面紙	(5) toilet paper	衛生紙	(6) soap dispenser	給皂機
(7) hand dryer	烘手機	(8) urinal	小便斗	(9) toilet	馬桶
(10) plunger	馬桶吸盤	(11) washbowl	洗臉盆	(12) toilet brush	馬桶刷

41

親子英文共讀筆記欄

可以把不熟悉的
單字片語寫在這邊喔！

Unit 3
虛榮的烏鴉

精選句型 spend money/time on...

主詞 + give + 物 + to + 人

make a plan to + V

片語解析 before long

文法解析 可數與不可數名詞

MP3★Track3

The Crow Full of Vanity

"You spent all of your pocket money again? Today is just Thursday for God's sake!"

這是「星期四」，記得 T 要大寫

Mama Crow gives Cody the little crow 1000 dollars once a week. But Cody likes to buy a lot of things. He

是「一次」的意思，「兩次」就是 twice。

usually spends his money on many kinds of colorful feathers. So, he always becomes poor **before long**.

有一句話說 "Birds of a feather flock together."，就是「物以類聚」的意思。

But this week, it seems he bought something

也可以寫成 he seemed to have bought

different.

Pause & Answer 動動腦

1. How often does Cody get his pocket money?
（寇弟多久拿一次零用錢？）

解答在 P.224

虛榮的烏鴉

「你又花光零用錢了？天啊！今天才星期四！」

烏鴉媽媽每星期給小烏鴉寇弟一千元，然而寇弟喜歡買很多東西。他通常把錢花許多種彩色的羽毛上。所以，他總是沒多久就變窮了。但這個星期他似乎買了不一樣的東西。

Keywords 關鍵字詞

1	vanity	[`vænətɪ]	adj.	虛榮
2	crow	[kro]	n.	烏鴉
3	spend	[spɛnd]	v.	花費
4	pocket money	[`pɑkɪt] [`mʌnɪ]	n.	零用錢
5	sake	[sek]	n.	理由
6	colorful	[`kʌləfəl]	adj.	彩色的
7	feather	[`fɛðə]	n.	羽毛
8	poor	[pʊr]	adj.	貧窮
9	before long	[bɪ`fɔr] [lɔŋ]	adv.	很快

colorful

feather

pocket money

充 電 站

for God's sake 是「我的天啊！」，通常放在句尾。至於大家熟悉的Oh! My God! 習慣上是擺在句子的開頭。比如說：What's wrong with you, for God's sake?（天啊！你是怎麼了？）就可以等於 "Oh my God/my goodness! What's wrong with you?" 不過，當 for God's sake 擺在句首時，那又是另外一回事囉！因為它帶有「拜託」的意思，表示「看在老天的份上」。比如說，"For God's sake, could you please slow down?"（拜託一下，你可以慢一點好嗎？）

"**Mom**, can I have more for my **pocket** money?" Cody

這個字是 mommy（媽咪）的簡寫　　　　　　　本來是「口袋」的意思

asked poorly.

"Where did your money go? NT$1000 dollars is not a

small amount," Mama Crow asked angrily.

這個small不可以用little取代喔

"I… I bought a bottle of mineral water, a **pair** of pearl

pair可以當動詞表示「成雙；成對」

earrings and a pack of cheese powder," Cody

replied.

"**What for?**" Mama Crow got even **angrier.**

等於 Why?　　　　　　　　　　　　　這是 angry 的形容詞比較級

"I… I want to make a lucky cake and give it to you,

mom."

Pause & Answer 動動腦

2. Why did Cody buy those things?

（寇弟為什麼要買那些東西？）

解答在 P.224

「媽，我可以再要一點零用錢嗎？」寇弟可憐兮兮地問。

「你把錢都花到哪裡去了？一千元可不是小數目！」烏鴉媽媽生氣地問。

「我……我買了一瓶礦泉水、一對珍珠耳環和一包起司粉」寇弟回答。

「你買這些東西要做什麼？」烏鴉媽媽更加生氣了。

「我……我想要做一個幸運蛋糕給你。」

Keywords 關鍵字詞

10	poorly	[`pʊrlɪ]	adv.	可憐地
11	amount	[ə`maʊnt]	n.	數量
12	bottle	[`bɑtḷ]	n.	瓶子
13	mineral	[`mɪnərəl]	n.	礦物
14	pair	[pɛr]	n.	成對
15	pack	[pæk]	n.	（一）包
16	earring	[`ɪr‚rɪŋ]	n.	耳環
17	powder	[`paʊdɚ]	n.	粉

pearl earring

bottle

powder

pocket 就是指衣服裡的「口袋」，而「口袋裡的錢」（pocket money）就是指父母給小孩的零用錢，但是可別跟用於一般公司行號的「零用金」petty cash 搞混了喔！另外，如果我們去買東西，店家找給我們的「找零」，可以用 change 表示。最後要注意的是，「錢」都是沒有複數形（不可以加 -s）的，千萬別寫成 moneys、cashes 或是 changes 囉！

"Oh dear, it's good if you want to buy me a present"

it 在這裡是代替後面的 if you want to⋯

Mom petted Cody's head.

"But $1,000 a week is quite enough for you."

這裡也可以說 per week（每週）

"So what should I do, mom?" Cody asked in a lower

這裡的 in 不是「在裡面」喔！表示「用⋯」聲音來說話。

voice.

"You have to learn how to make a plan to use your

記得喔！plan（計畫）的後面常常加 to

pocket money."

"No problem. I will do that. But, for now I still need a

多一個 for 是要特別強調「現在」就要。

dozen dinosaur tails. So can I have another 200

dollars now? "

Pause & Answer 動動腦

3. How much did Cody need for his mother's present?

（寇弟需要多少錢來買媽媽的禮物？）

解答在 P.224

「哦，親愛的，你想要買禮物給我是很好的事」烏鴉媽媽輕撫著寇弟的頭。

「不過一個星期一千元對你來說已經綽綽有餘了。」

「媽咪，那我該怎麼辦？」寇弟小聲地問

「你必須學會如何規劃使用你的零用錢。」

「沒問題，我會做到的，但我現在還需要一打的恐龍尾巴，所以可以再給我兩百元嗎？」

Keywords 關鍵字詞

18	present	[`prɛz(ə)nt]	n.	禮物
19	pet	[pɛt]	v.	撫弄
20	plan	[plæn]	n.	計畫
21	problem	[`prabləm]	n.	問題
22	a dozen	[ə `dʌzn̩]	adj.	一打；十二個
23	dinosaur	[`daɪnəˌsɔr]	n.	恐龍
24	tail	[tel]	n.	尾巴

present

tail

充電站

最後，雖然寇弟答應鴉媽以後會好好計畫零用錢的使用，但還是跟她「再要了兩百元」，要注意的是這裡的another用法。another 原本是「另一個」的意思，比如說，"Besides basketball, I have another hobby."（除了籃球，我還有個嗜好。）但"another 200 dollars" 可不能說成是「另一個兩百元」，而是「還要兩百元」。例如，Can I have another piece of cake?（我可以再要一塊蛋糕嗎？）另外，"One more, please."（麻煩再來一個。）也可用於類似情境中。

Useful Expressions 精選句型

spend money / time on… 把錢／時間花在…

→ You need to spend more time on your schoolwork.
　你得花更多時間在學校功課上。

主詞 + give + 物 + to + 人　給某人某物

→ My daddy gave a present to mom.
　= My daddy gave mom a present.
　我爸給了媽咪一個禮物。

make a plan to + V　計畫去做…

→ Let's make a plan to buy mom a surprise gift.
　我們來計畫為媽媽買一份驚喜的禮物。

Sentence Patterns 句型解析

- 無論是「花時間」或是「花錢」都可以用這個動詞喔!比如說:

  I spent NT$50 on this book.(我花了 50 元買這本書。)
  My teacher spent the time after school teaching me English.
  (我的老師在放學後還花時間教我英文。)

- give 這個動詞有點特別,因為它後面可以有兩個受詞,我們把它稱作「授予動詞」:

  I gave the lucky cake to my mom.(我把這幸運蛋糕給了媽媽。)
  = I gave my mom the lucky cakc.
  → "my mom" 和 "the lucky cake" 都是 gave 的受詞喔!

- 雖然有時候計畫趕不上變化,但是我們做事情還是得「有所計畫」(make a plan)才好。那麼,「計畫要做某事」就可以這麼說:

  You need to make a plan to study English.(你得開始計畫念英文了。)
  = You need to plan to study English.

我們出去玩囉!

YA!

Don't you make a plan?

before long

● 什麼叫作「在長長久久之前」啊？

大家都知道 before 是「在…之前」的意思，所以像 before dark（在天黑以前）、before day（在天亮之前）都是很好理解的片語，不過，before long 這個片語，正確理解它的意思是「在時間拉長以前」，就是「不會過太久」的意思囉！

Wow! They are dating! I think they must fall in love before long!
哇噢！他們在約會耶！我想他們很快就陷入熱戀了！

I hope to get home before dark.
（我希望在天黑之前回到家。）

● 那麼大家來猜猜看，after you 是什麼意思？不是「在你後面」喔！那是「您先請」的意思。

不…你先你先！

是你先來的嗎？

A: Are you the next one to be served?
（你是下一位點餐者嗎？）
B: No, after you.（不，您先請。）

可數與不可數名詞

現在把時光倒帶,場景拉回到幾天前,地點是寇弟的學校旁,在蟾蜍老闆經營的雜貨店中,寇弟手上正拿著幸運蛋糕的材料清單,問著老闆:「我要一瓶礦泉水、一對珍珠耳環、一包起司粉,以及一打恐龍尾巴。」(I want a bottle of mineral water, a pair of pearl earring**s**, a pack of cheese powder, and a dozen of dinosaur tail**s**.)。

當然,我們已經知道寇弟帶的錢不夠,所以才會有剛才的故事。不過接下來我們先來比較這幾樣東西:

a bottle of mineral water		a bottle of	mineral water
a pair of pearl earring**s**	→	a pair of	pearl earring**s**
a pack of cheese powder		a pack of	cheese powder
a dozen dinosaur tail**s**		a dozen	dinosaur tail**s**

眼尖的讀者馬上就會發現,水(water)和粉末(powder)的字尾沒有加s,而耳環和尾巴卻有加s,想想看這是為什麼?

乍看之下沒有甚麼不同,咦!好像有些東西不太一樣哦!

在這邊老師就先將最基本的概念灌輸給大家。我們在第一篇的時候有學過名詞的單複數概念，現在則是要告訴各位有關英文名詞的另一個祕密：可數和不可數。

其實，只要能夠清楚區分單數和複數，就可以了解這個東西到底是可以數還是不可數。如果是不可數的名詞，當然就不能有複數的型態出現。那麼，可數和不可數有什麼不一樣？顧名思義，不可數就是沒有辦法計算的東西，既然沒有辦法計算出數量，那怎麼會有單複數的問題？所以理所當然不用加s，前面也不會加上a或an等冠詞。而不可數名詞基本上可以分成三類，詳細分類可以參考以下表格。

專有名詞	人名：Chris、Jack、Zoe…
	地名：Taiwan（台灣）、Taipei（台北）、America（美國）…
	語言：English（英語）、Chinese（中文）…
	星期：Monday（星期一）、Tuesday（星期二）…
	節日：Christmas（聖誕節）、Chinese New Year（新年）…
物質名詞	食品材料：pork（豬肉）、rice（米飯）、bread（麵包）…
	物質材料：iron（鐵）、clothing（衣服）…
	液體：water（水）、tea（茶）…
	氣體：air（空氣）…
抽象名詞	time（時間）、help（幫助）、love（愛）

所以囉，如果要表達不可數名詞的數量，應該怎麼處理？其實答案已經出現在故事裡了。那就得在前面加上適當的單位，舉例來說，rice就可以說成是 a bowl of rice（一碗飯），麵包則可以說 a slice of bread（一片麵包）。

在「雜貨店」裡

　　有了足夠的錢以後，寇弟飛奔地又來到這家雜貨店（grocery），不過這個時候蟾蜍老闆正在忙，他要寇弟自己去找他要買的東西，大家一起來幫寇弟找找看吧！

(1) a glass of eyeballs	一杯眼球	(2) a smoking pipe	一支煙斗
(3) a toad	一隻蟾蜍	(4) boxes of magic beans	一盒盒的魔豆
(5) a dinosaur tail	恐龍尾巴	(6) bags of ash	幾袋灰燼
(7) a jar of honey	一罐蜂蜜	(8) a bottle of mineral water	一瓶礦泉水
(9) a pack of cheese powder	一包起司粉	(10) pearl rings	珍珠耳環

親子英文共讀筆記欄

可以把不熟悉的
單字片語寫在這邊喔！

Unit 4

塞翁失馬

精選句型	There be nothing but...
	On the way to + 地方, S +V…
	What would happen if + S + V…
片語解析	You never know!
文法解析	介系詞及其基本句型

Zeroun Lost His Horse

"Under the arch of the temple, look

它的複數形要加 – es，變成 arches 喔！

between the stone lions and your

horse is right next to the pine tree.

But after sunset there will be nothing by the

與它相對的就是 sunrise（日出）

tree." When Zeroun came back from work, there was

nothing but a strange note on the table inside the

這個but可不是「但是」的意思，而是「除了…之外」。

stable. "Oh no, my horse is missing again," he

thought. But this time, with this clue, he decided to

可以解釋為「因為有了…」

follow it.

Pause & Answer 動動腦

1. Where did Zeroun lose his horse?

（塞翁的馬在哪裡不見的？）

解答在 P.224

58

塞翁失馬

「寺廟的拱門之下，朝著石獅子的中間看過去，你的馬就在松樹的旁邊，但是日落之後，可就什麼都沒有了！」當塞翁工作回來，馬廄中除了一張放在桌上的奇妙紙條外，什麼也沒有。塞翁心想「不會吧！我的馬又不見了。」不過這次，既然有這個線索，他就決定一探究竟。

Keywords 關鍵字詞

arch

1	arch	[artʃ]	n.	拱門
2	temple	[`tɛmpl]	n.	寺廟
3	pine tree	[paɪn] [tri]	n.	松樹
4	sunset	[`sʌnˌsɛt]	n.	日落
5	strange	[strendʒ]	adj.	奇怪的
6	note	[not]	n.	字條
7	stable	[`stebl]	n.	馬廄；畜舍
8	clue	[klu]	n.	線索
9	follow	[`falo]	v.	追蹤

sunset

stable

充電站

「塞翁失馬，焉知非福」這句諺語相信大家都聽過，它的英文其實就是短短幾個字：a blessing in disguise。blessing 是動詞 bless 加 ing 之後轉成名詞的意思，解釋為「祝福」或「賜福」。而 disguise 是「偽裝」或「掩飾」的意思。那麼「掩飾的祝福」也就是說，一件看似倒楣的事情，結果帶來好運。就像這篇故事裡的賽翁一樣！

On the way to the temple, he saw a dragon. "Hi there,

Brother Dragon. Did you see my horse?" he asked.

"No, I didn't. By the way, can you give me a hand? I

不是「給我一隻手」，它是help的意思

can't find my cane, and I feel so weak without it."

有一種水果叫「甘蔗」，也是用這個字喔

"Sure!" Zeroun answered freely, although he was

kind of in a hurry. Zeroun was patient. He didn't hurry

注意 kind of 和 a kind of 意思可是差多囉   它還有一個意思，叫作「病人」

him. When they finally arrived at the temple, Zeroun

didn't see his horse beside the tree and the sun was

地球（earth）、月亮（moon）、太陽
（sun）這些字前面一定要有定冠詞 the 喔

sinking fast.

Pause & Answer 動動腦

2. What did the Dragon look for?

（龍大爺在找什麼？）

解答在 P.224

在前往寺廟的路上，他遇見了一條龍。塞翁問：「哈囉！龍兄，請問你有看見我那匹馬嗎？」龍兄回答：「不，我沒看見喔。對了，我可以請你幫一個忙嗎？我找不到拐杖，且我沒有拐杖的話，整個龍身就很虛弱。」雖然塞翁有點著急，不過還是豪爽地答應：「沒問題！」塞翁很有耐心。他並沒有催促他。當他們總算抵達寺廟時，太陽也快要下山了，但塞翁並沒有在樹旁看到他的馬。

Keywords 關鍵字詞

cane

10 dragon	[`drægən]	n.	龍
11 by the way		adv.	對了…；順道一提
12 cane	[ken]	n.	拐杖
13 weak	[wik]	adj.	虛弱
14 freely	[`frilɪ]	adv.	直爽地
15 kind of	[`kaɪnd‚əf]	adv.	有一點
16 patient	[`peʃənt]	adj.	有耐性的
17 hurry	[`hɝɪ]	v.	催促
18 sink	[sɪnk]	v.	下沉

hurry

patient

充電站

在這一段開頭，賽翁遇到龍兄時，他說「Hi, there, Brother Dragon.」這裡的 "Hi, there" 可不是要人家「看那裡」的意思喔！"Hi there" 就是個在國外很常見，但是在台灣的學校教室裡不常教的招呼用語，但它出現頻率卻很高喔。所以，不要只會說 "How are you?" 了！

"That's strange. It should be here..." He was

confused. "Forget it. Let me help him find his cane
　　　　　　　是「算了吧」，不是「忘記它」的意思喔！

first or he might die." But as he turned around, the

Dragon was gone and instead, his horse was standing
　　　　　gone 當形容詞用，表示「不見了」

right behind him. When he came home, he saw a

crowd standing in front of his house. It came down.
　　　　　也可以用原形stand，但不可以用to stand。

"What would happen if my horse was not missing...?"
　　　　　would 是 will 的過去式

he thought. A familiar voice came from Zeroun's back

and said "You never know!"
　　　　　　　　　這是個頻率副詞，但可用在「過去」、「現在」、「未來」式中

Pause & Answer 動動腦

3. What could happen to Zeroun if his horse was not
missing? What do you think?

（要是塞翁的馬沒有不見的話，會發生什麼事？你認為呢？）

解答在 P.224

62

他困惑地想著：「奇怪，應該是在這邊才對……」「算了，我還是先幫他找拐杖好了，不然他可能會死掉。」而正當塞翁轉過身，龍兄不見了，取而代之的竟然是他的馬。當他回家時，看見一群人站在他家門前。他的房子已經倒塌了。他想，「要是我的馬沒有不見的話……，那會怎樣？」塞翁的背後傳來一個熟悉的聲音說：「天知道！」

Keywords 關鍵字詞

19	confused	[kən`fjuzd]	adj.	困惑的
20	turn around	[tɜn] [ə`raund]	v.	轉過身
21	right behind...		prep.	就在…後面
22	instead	[ɪn`stɛd]	adv.	反而
23	crowd	[kraʊd]	n.	人群
24	come down	[`kʌm`daun]	v.	倒塌
25	familiar	[fə`mɪljɚ]	adj.	熟悉的
26	never	[`nɛvɚ]	adv.	絕不；從不

confused

turn around

充 電 站

voice 和 sound 最大的區別，就是「發聲者」是人還是物。比如：
Don't you think his voice sounds like his father's?（你不覺得他的聲音聽起來很像他爸爸的聲音嗎？）I was awakened by the sound of alarm clock.（我被鬧鐘的聲音叫起床了。）大家看出來了嗎？voice 其實就是指「人」所發出的聲音，比如說話、唱歌等；而 sound 是指各種聲響，包括生物與非生物。

Useful Expressions 精選句型

There be nothing but...
只有…；除了…什麼也沒有

→ There's nothing but a banana here for you!
這邊只有一根香蕉可以給你喔！

On the way to + 地方, S + V…
在…的路上，……

→ On the way to the station, it rained and the wind blew hard.
在前往車站的路上，風雨很大。

What would happen if + S + V... 如果…會怎樣？

→ What would happen if your ring fell into the ditch?
萬一妳的戒指掉入水溝裡怎麼辦？

● 這個句型是 there be…（有…）的延伸。比如說：There is a banana for you.（有一根香蕉可以給你。）那麼，這個例句就是在 be 動詞 is 後面，再加一個 "nothing but"，等於 only 的意思。

● 首先，on the way 就是「在路上」，而 way 後面的 to 是個介系詞，後面要接「地點」。而 way 後面也可以放「地方副詞」，比如 home 這個字就是。比如：on my way home 就是指「在我回家的路上」。

● "What would happen if…" 中的 "would happen" 是可以省略的，變成 "What if…?"，其實這是很常見的問句。比如說：

What would happen if an earthquake took place?
= What if an earthquake took place?（萬一發生地震時怎麼辦？）

片語解析

You never know!

● 什麼叫作「你絕對不知道！」？

You never know! 字面意義是，「你絕對不會知道！」其實它的意思是「誰知道啊！」、「天曉得！」或是「這很難說！」通常用在「令人難以預料」、「無法解釋」的情況，或是用來「鼓勵別人」的一句話。比如說：

A: That guy is so handsome and so popular among girls that I'm not likely to be his match.

A：那傢伙這麼帥又這麼受女生歡迎，我不可能是他的對手。

B: You never know. You could just be that girl's type.

B：這很難講。說不定你就正好是那女孩喜歡的類型。

A: He said that he has been to twenty countries!"

B: "You never know!"

A：「他說他去過二十個國家！」

B：「天知道！」

A: How did your interview go?
（你面試得怎樣？）

B: I think it went well, but you never know.
（我覺得很挺順利的，不過也很難說。）

66

介系詞及其基本句型

首先，我們回想一下那一張神祕到不行的字條，上面寫著……

"**Under** the arch of temple, look **between** the stone lions and your horse is right **next** to the pine tree. But **after** the sunset there will be nothing by the tree."

紅字的部分就是所謂的介系詞，大家是不是可以從中找出一些共同點呢？

沒錯，這些紅字所代表的意思，依序是：「在…下面 (under)」、「在…(兩者) 中間 (between)」、「在…旁邊 (next)」、「在…之後（after）」以及「在…一旁 (by)」。似乎都在表達「位置」，或「時間」。因此，我們可以得知介系詞的功能之一就是用來表示位置。那麼，大家可以再複習一下課文中出現過、表示「位置」的介系詞：

inside	在……裡面	…there is nothing but a mysterious note on the table **inside** the stable.
on	在……上面	…there is nothing but a mysterious note **on** the table inside the stable.
under	在……下面	**Under** the arch of the temple…
behind	在……後面	…his horse was standing right **behind** him.

in front of	在……前面	…a crowd standing **in front of** his house.
between	在……之間	…look **between** the stone lions…
next to	在……旁邊	…your horse is right **next to** the pine tree.

大家發現了嗎？有些介系詞的前面，都搭配了其它字詞，這就是介系詞的一個靈活的特性。不過，我們還是要知道它的基本句型：「主詞 + be + 介系詞 + 名詞」。

在這個故事中，我們可以看見許多介系詞，但有些讀者或許會問：「老師，我有看到很多介系詞啦，不過都只看到這個句型的一部分而已，這是怎麼一回事？」哈哈……沒關係，接下來老師就將這些句子都打回原形。

Under the arch of the temple…
→ It is under the arch of the temple.
…your horse is right next to the pine tree
→ Your horse is next to the pine tree.
…there is nothing but a mysterious note on the table inside the stable.
→ The mysterious note is on the table.
…his horse was standing right behind him.
→ His horse was behind him.
…a crowd standing in front of his house.
→ The crowd is in front of his house.

其實這些句子都是利用這個「介系詞的基本句型」，只是為了顧及故事性及語感，所以才要做出一些變化。

「十二生肖」的英文

　　小朋友！你知道自己是「屬」什麼生肖嗎？趕快找找自己的生肖是下面哪一隻動物吧！

(1) rat / mouse	鼠	(2) ox / bull / cow	牛	(3) tiger	虎
(4) rabbit	兔	(5) dragon	龍	(6) snake	蛇
(7) horse	馬	(8) goat / sheep	羊	(9) monkey	猴
(10) cock / rooster	雞	(11) dog	狗	(12) pig / swine	豬

親子英文共讀筆記欄

可以把不熟悉的
單字片語寫在這邊喔！

Unit 5
三隻小豬

精選句型 S + sound like + N

I'm sorry but...

take one's last sleep

片語解析 shake a leg

文法解析 現在進行式

Please stop getting angry!

道歉要有誠意!

MP3★Track5

Three Little Pigs

Piggy Piglet Pigo

"Come on, shake a leg! You have to…

什麼叫「搖動一條腿」？稍後「片語解析」告訴你喔！

ah… H…help me!!" Someone's

screaming on the phone.

中文說「在電話中」，英文要說 "on" the phone 喔！

"Who's calling? Hello, HELLO? Are you Pigo? Hello?"

A terrifying call awakened Piggy at midnight and it

還記得前面學過 wake up 這個片語嗎？

sounded like Pigo. So Piggy called him up in no time.

He wanted to make sure he's fine.

"Hello, I'm sorry for calling this late. Pigo, are you

這個 this 表示「這麼地」相當於 so

all right?"

「全對」嗎？又不是考100分！它等於 O.K.

Pause & Answer 動動腦

1. When did Piggy make a phone call to Pigo?
   （Piggy 在何時打電話給 Pigo？）

解答在 P.???

72

三隻小豬

　　「快！你得……啊……救……救命啊！！」某人在電話的另一頭尖叫著。

　　「是誰？喂，喂？是豬大哥嗎？喂？」

　　一通可怕的來電叫醒了半夜正在睡覺的豬老二，聽起來像是豬老大的聲音，所以豬老二立刻打了通電話給豬老大。他想確定他沒事。

　　「哈囉！不好意思這麼晚打來，豬老大你還好嗎？」

Keywords 關鍵字詞

1	shake	[ʃek]	v.	搖動，震動
2	scream	[skrim]	v.	尖叫
3	terrifying	[ˋtɛrə͵faɪɪŋ]	adj.	可怕的
4	midnight	[ˋmɪd͵naɪt]	n.	半夜
5	awaken	[əˋwekən]	v.	叫醒
6	call up	[ˋkɔl͵ʌp]	v.	打電話（給某人）
7	in no time	[ɪnˋno͵taɪm]	adv.	立刻
8	make sure	[ˋmek ʃur]	v.	確定（某件事情）

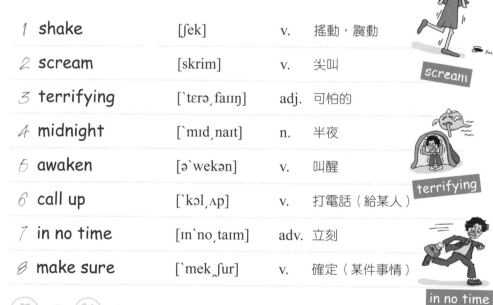

scream

terrifying

in no time

充電站

我們平常用中文打字聊天，或傳送訊息時，常常會用「呼~」、「呃…」、「蛤？」、「嗯…」之類的字眼來表達感覺。那麼如果用英文呢？比方說，ha 就是「哈」（笑聲），Nah 或 NAAAAHH，是「才沒有」、「才不是啊」的意思，而 Ouch! 是用來表達很痛、很糟糕的感覺，另外 Hmm… 也很常見，表示猶豫的聲音，可解釋為「呃…」。最後，像是 Shh!（噓）、Oops!（驚呼）以及課文一開始就看到的 Ah... 或 Ahhh...（啊），是可以廣泛使用在各種想要表達「大叫」的地方。

"Oops, I'm sorry, but he's not in right now. Could you

這個 in 是個副詞，表示「在裡面；在家裡」

please call back later?"

"OK! I'll do that in five minutes. Bye… Wait! Who's

this and where is Pigo?"

"You got me. I'm Wolf. Your brother is in my belly, and

有一點像中文的「被你發現了！」

you are the next!"

"Oh No! I must warn my little brother," Piggy thought.

知道 little 和 small 的差別嗎？little 用來形
容「活的」small 用來形容「非生命體」喔

Then, he tried to call Piglet by cellphone, but its

battery was dead. "What can I do? Wolf is

coming soon. Wait, maybe I can…"

還記得前面學過吧！不要說成 coming fast 喔！

Pause & Answer 動動腦

2. Who answered the phone made by Piggy?

（誰過來接豬老二打來的電話？）

解答在 P.225

「哎！抱歉，他現在不在，可以麻煩你晚一點再回電嗎？」

「好的，那我五分鐘之後再打。再見…等等！你是誰？豬老大咧？」

「被你發現了，我是大野狼，你哥哥現在在我的肚子裡，下一個就輪到你啦！」

「啊，不行！我得警告一下小弟，」豬老二心想。

然後，他試著用手機打電話給豬小弟，可是電池卻沒電了。

「我該怎麼辦？大野狼就要來了！等等，或許我可以……」

Keywords 關鍵字詞

9	call back	[`kɔl bæk]	v.	回電
10	minute	[`mɪnɪt]	n.	分鐘
11	wolf	[wʊlf]	n.	野狼
12	belly	[`bɛlɪ]	n.	肚子
13	next	[`nɛkst]	n.	下一個
14	warn	[wɔrn]	v.	警告
15	cellphone	[`sɛlfon]	n.	手機
16	battery	[`bætərɪ]	n.	電池
17	dead	[dɛd]	adj.	（電池）沒電的

belly

warn

battery

充電站

「電池沒電」，就是課文裡所講的 The battery is dead.，也可以說 The battery died. 那如果要表達的是「快沒電」呢？我們可以說 My cellphone battery is dying.（我的手機電池快沒電了）或是 My cellphone battery is low.。

Bang! Bang! Bang! "Open the door, Piggy. You are my

英文的狀聲詞，如果用中文來表達的話，就是「砰！砰！砰！」

main dish today!" Wolf is shouting and pounding on

the door. Later he broke into the house, and you know

這是 break 的過去式，過去分詞是 broken

what is going to happen, don't you?

Finally, Wolf came to Piglet's house, and as the door

collapsed, a "BANG" was heard. Then, Wolf took his

這是 hear 的過去式及過去分詞

last sleep. Piglet was standing behind the door with a

是「在…後面」的意思，相反詞是 in front of

gun and said "Pigo told me everything by LINE! RIP!"

Rest In Peace（安息）的縮寫。

Pause & Answer 動動腦

3. Who was Wolf's main dish?

（誰是野狼的主餐呢？）

解答在 P.225

砰！砰！砰！「豬老二，快把門打開，你是我今天的主菜！」大野狼正又吼又叫地猛敲著門。後來，他破門而入，大家都知道要發生什麼事了，對吧？

大野狼終於來到豬小弟的家，當門倒下的瞬間，傳來「砰」的一聲。只見大野狼倒地不起，而豬小弟出現在門後，手裡拿著一把槍。

他說：「豬老大已經用 LINE 告訴我一切了！安息吧！」

Keywords 關鍵字詞

18	bang	[bæŋ]	n.	轟的一聲
19	main	[men]	adj.	主要的
20	dish	[dɪʃ]	n.	一盤菜
21	pound	[paʊnd]	v.	重擊；連續敲打
22	break into	[`brekɪntu]	v.	闖入
23	finally	[`faɪnḷɪ]	adv.	最後
24	collapse	[kə`læps]	v.	倒塌

bang

collapse

充　電　站

當大野狼在門外對著豬老二喊著：You're my main dish today.（你是我今天的主餐），大家可別把dish這個字看成「盤子」了，因為大野狼不可能可以把盤子吞到肚子裡的。所以，大野狼已經告訴我們，dish就是「一道菜」，那麼「主要的一道菜」（main dish）然就是指「主菜」了。除了menu（菜單）這個字大家應該很熟了，其他用餐時也會聽到的「開胃菜」（appetizer）、餐後甜點（dessert）、飲料（beverage）這些關鍵單字也不妨一起學起來吧！

S + sound like +名詞（子句）
聽起來像是…

→ The boy's cheerful voice sounds like he's not
feeling tired at all.
這男孩愉悅的聲音聽起來好像他一點都不感
到疲累。

I'm sorry, but… 我很抱歉，因為…

→ I'm sorry, but there was traffic jam on the way here.
對不起啦！因為來這裡的路上塞車。

take one's last sleep 長眠不醒；辭世

→ The wolf took his last sleep after eating too much food.
野狼吃下太多食物之後就撐死了。

Sentence Patterns 句型解析

● sound 也可以當動詞表示「聽起來」。所以呢,它跟「看起來」(look)、聞起來(smell)、嘗起來(taste)… 這些一樣,都是「感官動詞」,後面可以接形容詞或是「like + 名詞」。不過比較特別的是,look like 和 sound like 後面都可以接一個句子。

● I'm sorry. 或是直接講 Sorry.,是大家再熟悉不過的道歉用語。但是在講了 sorry 之後呢?要進一步説明對不起人家的事由,習慣上就是要用 but 開頭,而不説 because…(因為…),但是這裡的 but 不必翻譯成「但是…」。比如説:

I'm sorry, but I can't agree with you.(抱歉,我無法同意你。)

● take one's last sleep 其實很容易理解,就是「睡最後一次覺」,也就是睡了就不會再醒來的意思,屬於英文裡的所謂「委婉語」。就像中文所講的「辭世」、「長眠」,或者高僧的「圓寂」等。

shake a leg

- 什麼叫作「搖動一條腿」？

leg 當然是「腿」的意思，而 shake 則是「搖動」。其實英文的「抖腳」就可以說 shake one's leg，不過，我們應該不會對人家說「來！抖腳吧」，頂多叫你不要抖腳，譬如說 Stop shaking your leg. 之類的。所以下次如果聽到 shake "a" leg，而不是 shake "your" leg 的話，那就是要你「趕快行動」的意思。另外，還有一個和 leg 一樣的習慣用語：pull one's leg（開某人玩笑）。大家可別以為是「扯後腿」喔！

Please shake a leg, boy! I can't wait.
小子！請快一點，我等不及了。

Don't pull my leg, OK.?
You said you want to sit
with me yesterday!
別開我玩笑了好嗎？你昨天說
想和我坐一起！

Wow! The net is almost broken. The
soccer player really showed great power
of his leg!
（哇噢！網子幾乎要破了！這名足球員真是好腿力！）

現在進行式

　　「現在進行式」，簡單說，就是「現在正在進行或發生」的事情。想像一下自己是豬老二，得知哥哥已經被大野狼吃掉，而大野狼正朝著自己家逼近，弟弟又毫不知情待在家中，沒有防備。當發現手機沒電時，更是緊張，這個時候，我們想到可以用LINE傳訊息給豬小弟，正當輸入訊息的時候，大野狼也正在門外嚷嚷著……

Wolf **is** com**ing**. (大野狼要來了！)

Wolf **is** shout**ing** and slam**ming** the door.
(大野狼正在門外又吼又叫地猛敲著門。)

　　這裡紅色字的部分就是「現在進行式」囉！我們現在來回想一下前面學過的「現在式」，然後看看下面四個中文句子：

他吃飯。
他在吃飯。
他還在吃飯。
他正在吃飯。

　　大家覺得這四個句子如何？越是往下的句子，越能給人「當下」的氣氛，也就是說，「進行式」是用來表示「正在做什麼事」的句型。

至於現在進行式要怎麼使用？句型的部分很簡單，就是：

主詞	be 動詞	-ing

例如：

1. He is swimming.
2. I am playing a TV game.
3. They are playing soccer.

　　大家發現到了嗎？這三個句子的 be 動詞有什麼特別的地方？它們隨著什麼東西在變化呢？沒有錯！主詞是第幾人稱，單數或複數，這在講現在式的時候都提到過了喔！還有還有，現在進行式真正令人抓狂的地方，就是後面的V-ing，「給動詞加上 ing 的尾巴」可不是想像的那麼簡單！還要講究規則咧。而基本規則有三種：

1. 大部分的動詞，只要在字尾上加上ing即可。
   例如：cry → crying；watch → watching
2. 動詞的字尾是e，且e不發音時，則把e去掉，加上ing，即為現在分詞。例如：close → closing；live → living
3. 動詞的字尾是「短母音＋子音」時，則重複字尾，再加上ing即為現在分詞。例如：sit → sitting；run → running。

「每一道菜」的英文

　　小朋友們！除了學習豬家三兄弟的臨危不亂之外，我們來從大野狼說出的 main dish（主菜）開始，來試試下面這張圖中，桌上餐點英文怎麼說吧！

(1) vegetables 蔬菜	(2) salad 沙拉	(3) fried noodles 炒麵
(4) roast chicken 烤雞	(5) a bowl of rice 一碗白飯	(6) steamed fish 蒸魚
(7) fried eggs 荷包蛋	(8) pizza 披薩	(9) soup 湯

親子英文共讀筆記欄

可以把不熟悉的
單字片語寫在這邊喔！

Unit 6
莊周夢蝶

Unit

6

MP3★Track6

Dream of a Butterfly

Morpheus is a butterfly. He lives in a

small garden behind an old
後面的old是母音開頭的，所以要用an，而不~

apartment. He likes to fly around the
記得前面學過的 turn around 嗎？around 有「繞圈圈」的意思

garden. Sometimes he likes to stop on the bench,

sometimes he enjoys resting on the fence but most

of the time, he likes to daydream on a lantana, his
day 就是「白天」，那麼 daydream 應該很好理解了吧

favorite flower. To him, it is so beautiful and graceful

that he often daydreams that he becomes a lantana,

resting and idling in an open field.
這邊 open 是「空曠的」，不是「打開」喔

1. Where is Morpheus' favorite place to take a rest?
   （阿莫最喜歡在哪裡休息一下？）

解答在 P.225

86

莊周夢蝶

　　阿莫是一隻蝴蝶，他住在一棟老舊公寓後面的小花園裡。他喜歡在花園裡四處飛來飛去。有時候他喜歡停在長凳上，有時候喜歡在籬笆上休息，不過大部分時候，他喜歡在他最愛的花朵 — 馬櫻丹 — 上做白日夢。對他來說，它是如此美、如此優雅，以至於他會夢見自己就是一株馬櫻丹，悠遊自在地徜徉在一片曠野中。

Keywords 關鍵字詞

1	butterfly	[`bʌtɚˌflaɪ]	n. 蝴蝶
2	garden	[`gɑrdn̩]	n. 花園
3	apartment	[ə`partmənt]	n. 公寓
4	bench	[bɛntʃ]	n. 長凳
5	rest	[rɛst]	v. 休息
6	fence	[fɛns]	n. 籬笆
7	graceful	[`gresfəl]	adj. 優雅的
8	idle	[`aɪdl̩]	v. 閒混，無所事事

fence

graceful

idle

sometimes（有時候）這個字很容易看得出來是 some 和 time 合成的，不過在英文裡，確實有 sometime、some time 以及 some times 的用法，很多人都會搞得一頭霧水呢！首先 some times 應該是最容易理解了，它就是「有幾次」的意思，而 sometime 就是「改天」，是指「在未來的某個時候」，最後，some time 表示「一些時間」或「一段時間」，因為時間（time）本來就是不可數的名詞，所以千萬別加上 -s 囉！如果是可以加 -s 的 time，那麼它一定是指「次數」了。

One day he (fell into) a deep daydream, so deep that

fell 是 fall 的過去式。「作夢」可以說 fall into a dream

he forgot he was a butterfly. In the dream, he became

a flower, not any other (kind of) flower, but his favorite

還記得第四單元出現過的 kind of 嗎？這邊的意思不一樣喔！

lantana. He was in a farm filled with lantanas. There

were (hundreds of) butterflies flying and wandering

如果是 thousands of... 就是「數以千計」的意思

above him. Sometimes the butterflies would rest on

his petals and sometimes they collected his nectar. "I

feel so happy and free." he talked to himself. He felt

so relaxed that he even forgot he was a lantana (too).

放在句尾的 too 就是「也…」的意思

Pause & Answer 動動腦

2. How did Morpheus feel in his deep daydream?

（阿莫在他那睡得很深的白日夢裡感覺如何？）

解答在 P.225

88

有一天他做了一個很深的白日夢，深到他忘了自己是一隻蝴蝶。在那夢中，他變成一朵花，不是任何其他種類的，就是他最愛的馬櫻丹。他身處在一個開滿馬櫻丹的農場，而在他的上頭有數以百計的蝴蝶正在飛舞徘徊。有時候，一些蝴蝶會在阿莫的花瓣上休息，而有時候會採集他的花蜜。他自言自語：「我覺得好快樂，好自由啊！」，他放鬆到甚至也忘記自己是一朵馬櫻丹了。

Keywords 關鍵字詞

9	favorite	[ˋfevərɪt]	adj.	最喜愛的
10	field	[fild]	n.	原野；場地
11	filled	[fild]	adj.	充滿的
12	hundred	[ˋhʌndrəd]	n.	（一）百
13	wander	[ˋwʌndɚ]	v.	流連，閒逛
14	petal	[ˋpɛt!]	n.	花瓣
15	collect	[kəˋlɛkt]	v.	收集
16	nectar	[ˋnɛktɚ]	n.	花蜜
17	relaxed	[rɪˋlækst]	adj.	放鬆的

filled

collect

relaxed

充　電　站

　dream 這個字可以當動詞，也可以當名詞喔！比如說，「我昨晚夢見自己變成一隻鳥。」可以說，I dreamed I became a bird last night. 也就是說，dream 的後面可以接一個完整句子。不過，它也可以接一個名詞，我們可以說，I dreamed a terrible dream.（我做了個可怕的夢）。所以這邊大家要注意喔，「做」了一個什麼夢，不可以用 make，也不可以用 do 這些動詞喔！

Oops, it's raining; everybody flew away. Drops of

cold and chill rain fell on his cheeks. Morpheus was

人有兩片 cheek，所以是可以加 -s 的，如果換成 on his face，face 就不能加 -s 囉

wakened by a fit of shower from his daydream. He is

是「陣雨」，如果是「暴風雨」可以用 storm

a butterfly now, a butterfly completely. "Is it just a

daydream? But It felt so real, just like what I feel right

「就像是⋯」後面當然是接名詞，而 "what I'm feeling⋯" 就是個名詞性質的句子

now. Which one is real?" he thought.

So, is he dreaming about being a flower or is he the

be + ing，在這裡也可以等於 becoming

dream of a flower?

Pause & Answer 動動腦

3. Why did Morpheus wake up from his daydream?
（為什麼阿莫會從他的白日夢中醒過來呢？）

解答在 P.225

哎喲！下雨了，大家都飛走了，一滴滴冰涼的雨水落在他的臉上。阿莫被一場雨從白日夢中喚醒，他現在是一隻蝴蝶，徹頭徹尾的一隻蝴蝶。「這真的只是一場夢嗎？但它感覺是如此真實啊，和我現在的感覺一樣。哪一個才是真的呢？」，他思考著。

所以，究竟是他夢到自己變成一朵花，或者他才是一朵花的夢呢？

Keywords 關鍵字詞

18	drop	[drɑp]	n.	一滴
19	chill	[tʃɪl]	adj.	冷颼颼的
20	cheek	[tʃik]	n.	臉頰
21	waken	[ˋwekən]	v.	喚醒
22	shower	[ˋʃaʊɚ]	n.	陣雨
23	a fit of...	[ə ˋfɪt əv]	ph.	一陣…
24	completely	[kəmˋplitlɪ]	adv.	全然地
25	real	[ˋriəl]	adj.	真實的

it 這個代名詞，常常用來表示天氣或時間。這邊來跟大家談談用在天氣的說法。It's raining. 是「下雨了」，可以用來回答 "How's the weather today?"（今天天氣如何？）。另外，我們也可以回答說 "It's a fine / nice / great day today."（今天天氣不錯。）如果要表示「晴朗」的天氣，可以說 "It's sunny."，如果要表示「天氣陰陰的」，就可以說 "It's cloudy."。

Useful Expressions 精選句型

so ... that ... 如此地⋯以致於⋯

→ The wind was so strong that the tree almost fell down.

風如此強勁，以至於這棵樹幾乎要倒了。

... not ... but ... 不是⋯，而是⋯

→ In the fable, the rabbit loses the race not because of his speed but because of his carelessness.

在寓言故事裡，兔子輸掉比賽不是因為他的速度，而是他的疏忽大意。

事情 + feel + adj. （某事物）給人某種感覺

→ The terrible situation felt really helpless.

這糟糕的情況令人感到相當無力。

Sentence Patterns 句型解析

● so... that...（如此地…以至於…）是個很常見的搭配用語喔！它和 "too... to..."（太…而不能…）都有表示「**前後因果**」的意味。比方說，The news is too good to be true.（這消息太棒了，不太像是真的）。我們也可以說 "The news is so good that it doesn't sound true."。

● not 和 but，也是常見的搭配詞語，而且可連接**對等的詞句**。比如說，The one I like is **not** you, **but** him.（我喜歡的人不是你，而是他。）這裡的 you 和 him 都是人稱代名詞的受格。

● 本來 feel 這個動詞應該是給「人」用的（主詞應該是「人」），不過它也可以用在主詞是「事物」的時候。比方說，Wow! Your hair **feels** so smooth.（噢！你的頭髮感覺起來很柔順耶！）那麼，大家來練習一下這一句要怎麼說囉：這男孩聊得如此開心，以至於忘了該上床睡覺了。

_____

_____

解答在 P.225

嗄！
去睡覺啦！

talk to oneself

● 什麼叫作「和自己對談」？

這應該是個很好理解的片語吧！"talk to you" 就是「跟你說話」，不過如果是 "talk with you"，就比較偏向於「聊天」的意思。就像故事的最後，徬徨的阿莫，對於自己的夢，很正經地喃喃自語著。

A: I can't hear you clearly. Would you please say again?
我聽不太清楚耶！可以請你再說一次嗎？

B: Nothing. I'm just talking to myself.
沒什麼。我只是喃喃自語。

Sometimes we need to practice talking to ourselves.
「練習」這個動詞後面要接 Ving 喔
有時候我們需要練習和自己對話。

Hey, man! Come here, please. I need to talk to you.
喂，先生！請過來這裡一下。我要和你談談。

第三人稱單數

嗯……很奇妙的感覺，不是嗎？不知道大家是否也做過類似的白日夢？從一個十分逼真的夢中清醒，不禁自問：到底剛才的是夢還是真實，還是人生如夢？

這是改編自莊子的《齊物論》，算是一篇幻想色彩相當濃厚的作品，不過就在我們玩味其中的玄機之時，不知道有沒有注意到本篇故事的寫作方式和其他篇非常不同。除了沒有對話之外，全篇都是以旁觀者的角度來敘述，也就是說，是以第三人稱的角度來描寫。所謂的第三人稱單數，就是除了我（第一人稱單數）或你（第二人稱單數）之外的那「一個」人或物。簡單來說就是中文裡的「ㄊㄚ」：

he	she	it	the boy	the girl	the dog
他	她	它	男孩	女孩	狗兒

既然已經了解第三人稱單數是什麼東西，現在就來介紹它的規則吧！只要主詞是第三人稱單數，動詞簡單式的字尾後面都要加上 s。「那麼老師，字尾後面本來就有 s 的要加什麼？」嗯，大家反應很快！其實第三人稱加 s 的規則還挺多的，不過別擔心！老師已經整理好一個表格給大家參考：

字尾是……	要加什麼？	像這些字
s		passes
x		fixes
z	es	buzzes
sh		finishes
ch		catches
o		goes
子音+y	去 y 加 ies	flies
母音+y	s	plays

其他的動詞就直接加 s！

接著我們就來試試看如何運用第三人稱單數的句子吧！

他每天搭火車去上學。

He goes to school by train every day.

go，o 字尾是要怎麼變化？（趕快偷看一下上面吧！）
沒錯，是要加es

The boy exercises every morning.

並不是一定要看到「ㄊㄚ」才是第三人稱單數，只要是相同的概念都算是喔！

順道一提，have 的第三人稱單數形可不是 haves，而是 has，而 be 動詞的第三稱單數就是 is。

字詞一籮筐

各種「昆蟲」的英文

當阿莫正在花園做著他的白日夢時，還有其他許多小昆蟲（insect）前來這邊逗留玩耍，就像下面這張圖的情景一樣。現在我們就一起來找出下面每一隻會飛或不會飛的蟲蟲英文名字吧！

(1) dragonfly 蜻蜓	(2) butterfly 蝴蝶	(3) mosquito 蚊子
(4) bee 蜜蜂	(5) cockchafer 金龜子	(6) fly / housefly 蒼蠅
(7) flying moth 飛蛾	(8) cockroach 蟑螂	(9) grasshopper 蚱蜢

親子英文共讀筆記欄

可以把不熟悉的
單字片語寫在這邊喔！

Unit 7

朝三暮四

精選句型 can't wait to-V

do nothing but + V

need A to do B

片語解析 put oneself in other's shoes

文法解析 未來簡單式

Don't waste time watching TV, OK.?

Chop and Change

"Come on, monkeys! Have some yummy

have 也有「吃」（eat）的意思，例如：have breakfast（吃早餐）

bananas for dessert."

"Hooray! we can't wait to eat!"

Every morning and evening, all the

monkeys in Draco's circus would jump up and

通常是指「用兩隻腳跳」，如果是「單腳跳」就是用 hop 這個字

down, singing and dancing for the happiest moments

of the day: DESSERT TIME. But today, Draco said

something really disappointing.

表示「（某事物）令人失望」，如果是「（人）感到失望」就要用 disappointed

"Monkeys, go wash your hands first." Draco yelled.

" How many bananas will we have today?" Dax, the

how many…（有多少…）後面要接可數名詞。而後面接不可數名詞的是 how much

leader of the monkeys, asked Draco.

1. When is the happiest time for the monkeys?

（猴兒們最快樂的時光是在什麼時候？）

解答在 P.225

100

朝三暮四

「來吧！猴子們！快來吃好吃的香蕉點心吧！」

「呀呼！我們等不及要來吃囉！」

每天早上和傍晚時，所有在狙公馬戲團裡的猴子們會又蹦又跳、又是唱歌又是跳舞來迎接這一天之中最快樂的時刻：點心時間。但是，今天狙公說了些令人相當失望的話。

狙公喊著：「猴兒們，先去把手洗乾淨吧！」

猴子的頭頭德克斯問狙公說：「我們今天可以拿到幾根香蕉呢？」

Keywords 關鍵字詞

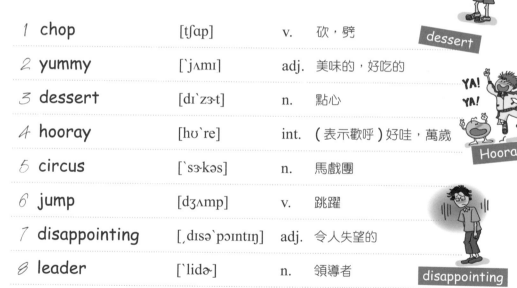

1	chop	[tʃɑp]	v.	砍，劈
2	yummy	[`jʌmɪ]	adj.	美味的，好吃的
3	dessert	[dɪ`zɝt]	n.	點心
4	hooray	[hʊ`re]	int.	（表示歡呼）好哇，萬歲
5	circus	[`sɝkəs]	n.	馬戲團
6	jump	[dʒʌmp]	v.	跳躍
7	disappointing	[ˌdɪsə`pɔɪntɪŋ]	adj.	令人失望的
8	leader	[`lidɚ]	n.	領導者

dessert

YA!
YA!

Hooray!

disappointing

充 電 站

《朝三暮四》這則寓言故事的英文名叫作 Chop and Change，而 chop 是一個動詞，表示「砍」或「劈」的意思，change 是「改變」。兩個動詞用 and 連接起來後，表示在同一時間有這兩個動作，所以呢，「砍了之後馬上又改變」的意思，不就是指「朝三暮四」、「三心兩意」嗎？在英文裡，"chop and change" 也變成了一個片語，而且特別設計兩個 ch- 開頭的動詞，念起來是不是也挺順口的呢？

"Well...I've recently been a bit needy." answered

相當於 a little，或是前面學過的 kind of

Draco, feeling embarrassed.

"So, to save some money, you'll have fewer bananas.

to + V 表示「為了…」，所以這裡不可以用 saving some money...

There will be three in the morning and four in the

evening. "

Then the monkeys can do nothing but accept it. After

one week, Dax went to talk to Draco about the

bananas.

"Draco, can we have some more bananas. We've

中文說的「再多一些…」，英文就是 some more，而不是 more some... 喔

been so hungry these days" Dax asked.

"Not today, my dear friend. Besides, eating too much

這邊的 Not 省略掉很多字喔！它等於 "I cannot give you more bananas..."

is not healthy." Draco said.

Pause & Answer 動動腦

2. How many bananas can the monkeys eat a day?

（猴兒們一天可以吃到幾根香蕉？）

解答在 P.225

狙公覺得有點不好意思，並回答說：「這…我最近有一點窮。」

「所以為了能省一點錢，你們的香蕉要減少些…以後你們早上只有三根香蕉，到了傍晚則有四根香蕉。」

於是猴兒們也只能接受了。一個星期後，阿德去找狙公談談香蕉的事情。

阿德問：「狙公，可以給我們多一點香蕉嗎？這幾天我們都快餓扁了。」

狙公說：「今天不行啊，親愛的朋友！況且，吃太多也不健康啊！」

Keywords 關鍵字詞

9	needy	[`nidɪ]	adj.	貧窮的
10	embarrassed	[ɪm`bærəst]	adj.	尷尬的
11	save	[sev]	v.	節省
12	few	[fju]	adj.	少的
13	accept	[ək`sɛpt]	v.	接受
14	hungry	[`hʌŋgrɪ]	adj.	飢餓的
15	besides	[bɪ`saɪdz]	adv.	此外
16	healthy	[`hɛlθɪ]	adj.	健康的

needy

embarrassed

healthy

充電站

英文裡的 morning、afternoon、evening 前面要用 in 還是 on？常常是讓初學者搞得一團亂的東西！其實大家只要記住一個原則，如果這三個字前面有形容詞或名詞，比如說，Sunday morning（星期日早上）、carefree afternoon（悠閒的下午），前面就要用介系詞 on，否則一律要用 in 囉！另外，night（夜晚）前面就不加 the，而直接用介系詞 at。

"Oh, please ! Put yourself in our shoes. We need

這邊的 please 是「拜託」，而不是「請」的意思

energy to do all of our tricks..." Dax begged.

"OK. Then, let me give each of you four in the

還記得 give 的用法嗎？它後面有兩個受詞喔！

morning and three in the evening, OK?" Draco asked.

"Let me think about it... I think that's an excellent

think 不要和 thank（謝謝）搞混囉！think about 有「考慮」的意思

idea." Dax answered heartily.

So the monkeys now can have one more in the

morning and three in the evening. And they are really

always happy about that.

be happy about... 表示「對…感到心滿意足」

Pause & Answer 動動腦

3. Why do the monkeys need these bananas?

（這些猴兒為什麼需要這些香蕉？）

解答在 P.225

阿德懇求說：「喔！拜託！站在我們的立場想想吧！我們需要體力來表演這些絕活啊！

狙公問：「好吧！那麼我早上給你們每一位四根，然後晚上三根，如何？」

「讓我想一下……我想這主意還不錯！」阿德開心回答。

所以，現在猴子們早上可以多吃一根香蕉，傍晚則有三根可吃。而且他們對於這結果確實感到滿意。

Keywords 關鍵字詞

17	energy	[ˋɛnə·dʒɪ]	n.	體力，能量
18	trick	[trɪk]	n.	花招，特技
19	beg	[bɛg]	v.	懇求
20	morning	[ˋmɔrnɪŋ]	n.	早上
21	evening	[ˋivnɪŋ]	n.	下午
22	excellent	[ˋɛksḷənt]	adj.	絕佳的
23	heartily	[ˋhɑrtɪlɪ]	adv.	開心地
24	really	[ˋrɪəlɪ]	adv.	真地

beg

excellent

充 電 站

have 這個動詞，最常出現的意思就是「有」。不過，在這個單元，have 是用來表示 eat（吃）。比如說，have lunch（吃午餐）。另外，它也可表示「喝」，我們可以說 "Let's have a cup of coffee."（我們去喝杯咖啡。）但必須注意的是，當「有」的意思時，沒有進行式（V-ing）喔！所以，如果要表示「我現在有一支新手機」我們不可以說 "I am now having a new cellphone."，要說 "I have a new cellphone now."。

105

人 + can't wait to + 原形V 等不及要…

→ The kids can't wait to have the delicious meal.
孩子們等不及要吃這一頓美食了。

do nothing but + V 只能（乖乖地）…

→ He's got a gun! I can do nothing but give him the money.
他有槍。我只能乖乖把錢給他了。

need A to do B 需要 A 來做 B

→ You need some courage to do that.
你需要一些勇氣來做那件事。

● can't wait 就是「迫不及待」，是用來表示「渴望或期待」的常見用語。不過必須注意的是，動詞 wait 後面必須用「to + 原形 V」，而沒有 "I can't wait doing that." 的說法喔！不過，我們倒是可以說，"I can't wait for your coming."（我等不及你的到來。）

● 還記得我們在第四單元學過的 There is nothing but...（只有…）這個句型嗎？當時的那個 but 是介系詞，表示「除了…之外」，後面要接名詞。而這邊的 but，是「對等連接詞」，所以它後面要用原形動詞 do。

● 「需要…」和「去做…」是前後兩個動作（不是同時發生的），所以第二個動作就要用不定詞的 to-V 來表示喔！那在什麼樣的情況下是兩個動作同時發生呢？比如說，「我有聞到浴室裡發出來的惡臭。」，就可以說 I smelled something stinking in the bathroom. 這時候就不能用 I smelled something to stink in the bathroom.（Ｘ）喔！

Put yourself in one's shoes

● 什麼叫作「把你自己放到某人的鞋子裡」？

這句話的意思當然不是叫我們真的把一個人塞到鞋子裡（太可怕了吧！），而是要從對方的角度去思考事情，也就是「設身處地為他人著想」，就如同把自己的腳放進別人濕漉漉的鞋子裡後，才能知道那感覺有多難受。另外，從 put oneself 延伸出來的片語，還有很常見的 put yourself at risk（將自己置於險境）以及 put oneself out for...（努力爭取…）。

Try to put yourself in his shoes, and you'll know how he feels.
試著站在他的角度去想，你就會知道他的感受了。

Don't put yourself at risk by doing that bare-handed.
別徒手做，那會將自己置入險境的。

People will naturally put themselves out for life in danger.
人們在危險時很自然地為極力求生存。

未來簡單式

　　本篇故事中的猴子真好笑！還不是一樣一天 7 根……其實這故事是要告訴我們，做人要有遠見，不要短視近利。也就是要能考慮到「未來」的事情。講到未來的事情，正好符合我們的文法主題：未來簡單式，顧名思義，就是用來敘述未來有可能發生的事情，而要造一個未來簡單式的句子只需要用到一個字：will。只要把 will 放在句子中動詞的前面就行了，但要注意一些小細節喔！老師先賣個關子，用以下幾個句子來看看是否可以觀察到這些規則：

現在簡單式： They have a lot of bananas. 他們有很多香蕉。		They will have a lot of bananas. 他們將會有很多香蕉
He has many bananas. 他有很多香蕉。		He will have many bananas. 他將會有很多香蕉
He is a banana master. 他是香蕉達人。	→ 未來式	He will be a banana master. 他將會成為香蕉達人
過去式： He had lots of bananas. 他曾經有很多香蕉。		He will have lots of bananas. 他將會擁有很多香蕉
現在進行式： He is eating a pile of bananas. 他正在吃一堆香蕉		He will eat a pile of bananas. 他將會吃一堆香蕉

除了把 will 丟到動詞前面外，動詞本身有什麼改變嗎？沒錯，全部都被打回「原形」了，無論是第三人稱單數動詞後的 -s、過去式動詞或者是現在進行式的動詞字尾 -ing，在 will 的後面都一律變回原形動詞，所以，我們只要能記住這兩件事情：

1. 將 will 放在動詞的前面。
2. 把動詞打回原形。

而在英語表達方式中，將兩個單字縮寫在一起是很常見的。例如 I am 縮寫成 I'm，you are 縮寫成 you're。而 will 也常和它前面的主詞或名詞縮寫在一起。也就是：

I will... = I'll...	Mary will... = Mary'll...
You will... = You'll...	They will... = They'll...
He / She will... = He'll / She'll...	There will be... = There'll be...
I will not... = I won't...　→ I'll not... (X)	

這邊要注意的是，在**否定**用法中，will not 等於 won't，但 will 不可先與前面的名詞縮寫後，再加 not。

最後，要特別一提的是，「be going to + 原形動詞」的用法。be going to 看起來像是現在進行式，比如說 I'm going to the train station.（我正要到火車站去。）

但如果 to 後面是動詞的話，那麼 be going to 就**很接近 will** 了，它用來表達「即將發生的狀態」。比如：

I **am going to** eat the meal.（我就要吃這頓飯了。）

「情緒表現」的英文

　　小朋友們，上完今天這一課，會不會覺得猴子德克斯是餓到昏頭了呢？不管怎樣，我們還是學到了「飢餓的」這個形容詞，那麼大家來找看看，下面哪一張圖是在表現「飢餓」，哪一張圖是「口渴」呢？

(1) hungry 飢餓的	(2) thirsty 口渴的	(3) hot 熱的
(4) cold 冷的	(5) noisy 吵鬧的	(6) sleepy 想睡的
(7) quiet 安靜的		

親子英文共讀筆記欄

可以把不熟悉的
單字片語寫在這邊喔！

鄉下老鼠與城市老鼠

精選句型	S + come into one's mind
	Would you like + N / to-V
	have a great time
片語解析	What's up?
文法解析	助動詞

MP3 ★ Track8

Country Mouse and City Mouse

Kert is a mouse and he lives in a far

country. One day, he invited his friend,

這個字也有「國家」、「故鄉」的意思

Rich, a mouse from a big city, to have

a get-together in his house. "What's up?" Kert

本來 get together (聚在一起)

greeted Rich happily. "Couldn't be better!" Rich

句首省略了 It。It couldn't be better. 字面意思是「沒有辦法再更好了。」那不就是「好得不得了」嗎?

answered gently. "Well, let's go down to my place! I

my place 就是 my home、my house (我家) 的意思

prepared lots of good stuff for you!"

When Rich heard "good stuff," images of steaks,

caviar, salmon and mutton came into his mind. But,

that's not the case...

Pause & Answer 動動腦

1. How does Rich feel when seeing the stuff on the table?

（當瑞奇看到桌上的東西時有什麼感覺呢？）

解答在 P.225

114

鄉下老鼠與城市老鼠

　　科特是一隻老鼠，他住在一個遙遠的鄉下，有一天他邀請他的朋友瑞奇 — 來自大城市的老鼠 — 過來他家聚一聚。科特高興地和瑞奇打招呼：「最近好嗎？」瑞奇溫和地回答：「好極了！」「嗯，咱們下去我的住處吧，我為你準備了很多好東西喔！」當瑞奇聽到「好東西」這幾個字的時候，浮現在他腦海的是牛排、魚子醬、鮭魚或羊肉之類的。可是，事情並非如此 ...

Keywords 關鍵字詞

1	far	[fɑr]	adj.	遠的
2	country	[`kʌntrɪ]	n.	鄉下
3	invite	[ɪn`vaɪt]	v.	邀請
4	get-together	[`gɛttə͵gɛðɚ]	n.	聚會
5	greet	[grit]	v.	打招呼
6	gently	[`dʒɛntlɪ]	adv.	溫和地
7	prepare	[prɪ`pɛr]	v.	準備
8	stuff	[stʌf]	n.	東西，物品
9	image	[`ɪmɪdʒ]	n.	影像

invite

greet

stuff

充電站

mouse（注意複數形為 mice）和 rat 都是「老鼠」，那麼兩者有何不同呢？通常 rat 比 mouse 要大。而另一個重要差別存在於文化中。西方人都以負面意義來使用 rat。有一個片語叫作 smell a rat，這可不是「聞到一隻老鼠」，而是「覺得不對勁」。mouse 則經常被賦予「寵物」，或「可愛」的象徵，所以米老鼠的英文是 Mickey Mouse，而不是 Mickey Rat 囉！

"Help yourself! Would you like some fish eye balls?"

「幫助你自己」其實就是「（別客氣）自己來」的意思

Kert said. "Yucky, it has strong smell of fish. No,

smell除了有「味道」，也可以用來表示「臭味」，通常是指食物的臭味

thanks." Rich answered. "Don't be so picky. Try some.

It's delicious." Kert insisted. "OK. Mmm... It tastes

還記得前面學過哪個字也是「美味的」？沒錯，是yummy喔！

amazing." Rich said. "And now I'm thirsty. May I have

some wine or champagne?" Rich asked.

「香檳」這個字和champion（冠軍）可以一起記下來吧
──「獲得冠軍開香檳慶祝」

"Come on! We aren't in the city. What about some

sugar cane juice? I made it myself." Kert passed the

「拐杖」這個字，前面出現過這個字喔！

juice to Rich.

Pause & Answer 動動腦

2. What drink did Kert give Rich?

（科特給了瑞奇什麼飲料？）

解答在 P.225

科特說：「自己來，別客氣！要來一些魚眼睛嗎？」瑞奇回答：「唉唷…魚腥味好重。不了，謝謝。」科特堅持說：「別挑食啦！吃吃看，這很好吃耶！」瑞奇：「好吧…嗯…想不到還滿好吃的。」他接著又問：「我口渴了。可以來點紅酒或香檳嗎？」

「拜託！我們又不是在城市裡，要不要喝點甘蔗汁？我自己做的。」柯特把果汁遞給瑞奇。

Keywords 關鍵字詞

10	yucky	[`jʌkɪ]	adj.	噁心的
11	strong	[strɔŋ]	adj.	強烈的
12	picky	[`pɪkɪ]	adj.	挑剔的
13	delicious	[dɪ`lɪʃəs]	adj.	美味的
14	insist	[ɪn`sɪst]	v.	堅持
15	taste	[test]	v.	嘗起來
16	amazing	[ə`mezɪŋ]	adj.	令人驚奇的
17	thirsty	[`θɝstɪ]	adj.	口渴的
18	champagne	[ʃæm`pen]	n.	香檳

yucky

delicious

amazing

Come on! 這個片語好常出現啊！它是「快點來！」、「別這樣！」、「少來啦！」？這些意思都沒錯。比方說，Come on! Let's go!（快點！我們走吧！）另外，當我們要安慰人家時，可以說 Come on! Cheer up!（別這樣了！振作點！）那如果是對於對方過分謙虛講的話不以為然，就可回應說 Come on! Don't be so humble!（少來這套！別這麼謙虛！）

"Wow! What a nice drink!" Rich said in surprise.

相當於 surprisingly (驚訝地)

Then Rich stuffed himself on everything on the table,

stuff oneself on + 食物 → 讓自己「大快朵頤」一番

and he said, "Although you don't have steak or salmon, these foods are just as good as them." Then they had a great time and talked a lot about their life

相當於 much，a lot of... (很多的...)

in the city and in the country.

"By the way, what's the black thing in the soup?" Rich asked curiously.

"What?! I didn't put anything black... Oops! It's a

表示「糟糕！」、「哎呀！」、「完蛋了！」等狀聲詞

cockroach!"

Pause & Answer 動動腦

3. What did Rich think about the foods in the country?
（瑞奇覺得這些鄉下食物如何？）

解答在 P.225

118

瑞奇驚訝地說：「哇噢！很棒的飲料耶！」然後瑞奇開始將桌上所有東西大快朵頤了一番，而且他說「雖然你這裡沒有牛排或鮭魚，不過這些食物還一點都不遜色呢！」於是他們玩得很愉快，且聊了許多關於他們在城市和鄉下的生活。

瑞奇好奇地問：「對了，剛才在湯裡面那個黑黑的東西是什麼啊？」「什麼？！我沒放什麼黑色的東西啊⋯ 糟糕！不會是蟑螂吧！」

Keywords 關鍵字詞

19	drink	[drɪŋk]	n.	飲料
20	surprise	[sə`praɪz]	n.	驚奇
21	stuff	[stʌf]	v.	使飽食；使吃得很飽
22	table	[`tebl̩]	n.	桌子
23	soup	[sup]	n.	湯
24	black	[blæk]	adj.	黑色的
25	curious	[`kjurɪəs]	adj.	好奇的
26	cockroach	[`kak͵rotʃ]	n.	蟑螂

stuff

curious

充電站

一般形容詞都是放在名詞前面，比如說「黑色的鞋子」（black shoes）、「漂亮的衣服」（beautiful clothes）。不過，這段出現了 something black 這個「名詞 + 形容詞」的組合，這叫作「形容詞的後位修飾」，聽起來很專業，很討厭吧！反正只要記得，碰到 something、anything、nothing、everybody⋯ 這類代名詞時，它們的形容詞一定要放在後面喔！比如：something special（特別的東西）、nothing wrong（沒有不對勁的事）⋯等。

Useful Expressions 精選句型

S+ come into one's mind　某人想到…

→ Something interesting came into his mind
　during the meal.
　在用餐時，他想到一件有趣的事。

Would you like + N / to-V…　您要不要…

→ Would you like | some curry?
　　　　　　　　 | to eat some curry?
　您要不要來點咖哩？

have a great time　玩得開心

→ I went to picnic last weekend and had a great time.
　我上週末在野餐上玩得很開心。

● 這個句型就等於「think of/about + 名詞」。所以這個例句就可以改成 He thought of something interesting during the meal.

● Would you like... 比起 Do you want... 是比較客氣的問法。另外，當我們要請求人家協助一件事時，也會用「Would/Could you please + 原形 V …」來詢問。

● 這句話也可以拿來當作「祝福語」。比如說，當你知道朋友要去哪裡旅行時，除了說聲「一路順風」(Have a nice trip.)，也可以再加一句 "Have a great time!"。

最後，大家來練習一下這句話的英文怎麼說吧：

「當他看到提款機時，就想到搶劫要發生了。」

When he saw the ATM machine, images of _____.

解答在 P.225

片語解析

What's up?

● 「什麼東西起來了？」這是什麼意思？

"What's up?"（近來如何？）是常見的打招呼用語，相當於 "How are you lately?"、"What's going on?"。有時候，它相當於 Hi! 或 Hello! 這類打招呼用語。這時候不一定要回答什麼 "Recently, I…"（最近，我 ...）。可以直接用同樣的話回覆，或者回答 Good!、Nice! 即可。那要是過得還不錯，就可以回答 "Couldn't be better!"。要是過得很普通，也可以回答 "Nothing special!"。

A: Hey man! What's up?
B: Just fine. And you?

A：喂，老兄！最近如何？ B：還不錯。你呢？

- -

I think my performance
couldn't be better!

這句話也可以用來表示讚美喔！

我覺得我的表演真是太棒了！

- -

A: Thank you for your treat. 感謝你的招待。
B: Nothing special. Just some home-
cooked dishes!

沒什麼啦！只是幾道家常菜而已！

助動詞

我們再來回顧一下鄉下鼠招待城市鼠時所問的那句話：Would you like some...。為什麼又要特地提到這句呢？沒錯！關鍵就在 would 這個字，它是個「助動詞」。

其實我們在第一單元時，就出現過助動詞了：當公雞對祖逖説 You will be late for school. (你上學會遲到的。) 這也是上個單元的文法重點：未來簡單式。而 will 就是一個「助動詞」。

記住！助動詞後面的動詞一定要用「原形」

所以呢，助動詞顧名思義就是用來輔助動詞的詞，在肯定句中，放在動詞前面，也可以形成「疑問句」和「否定句」。例如：

助動詞	功能	例句
do / does / did	形成問句	Where **do** you live? 你住在哪裡？
	形成否定句	He **does**n't / **does** not like you. 他不喜歡你。
	強化語氣	She **does** like you. 她的確喜歡你 She **did** say she likes me. 她的確説過喜歡我。
	代替前面出現過的動詞	He walks faster than she **does**.

※ 除了「強化語氣」的用法外，這邊的 do、does、did 不具任何意義。

除了上面介紹過的 do、does、did 等助動詞之外，還有一種助動詞，是放在動詞前面，用來表示「允許、推測、可能、未來、必須、義務、想要、請求」等，我們稱之為「情態助動詞」。常見的有：can / could / may / might / will / would / must / shall / should (= ought to) 等。我們用下面這個表來看就一目了然囉！

助動詞	表達意思	例句
can / could	可能、推測、允許、請求 ※ **could** 是 can 的過去式	1. The job **can** be finished before the weekend.（這工作可能可以在週末前完成。） 2. **Could** you tell me the truth?（可以請你告訴我事實嗎？）
may / might	可能、請求、允許 ※ **might** 是 may的過去式，具有相同意思，但語氣更帶有「婉轉」、「遲疑」。	1. She **may** be a nurse.（她可能是一位護士） 2. He **might** understand that.（他可能會理解那件事！）
will / would	未來、推測、請求 ※ **would** 是 will 的過去式	1. I said he **would** come!（我就說他會來嘛！） 2. **Would** you please close the window?（可以請你將窗戶關上嗎？）
shall/ should	應該、義務 ※ should = ought to	You **should** do as your teacher said.（你應該照老師說的去做。）
must / have to	必須、推測	1. You **must** do what your teacher says.（你必須照老師說的去做。） 2. She **must** be over 20 years old.（她肯定超過 20 歲了。）

表示「方位」和「位置」的英文

　　回想一下，一開始的 "… he lives in a far country."，還有，當科特對著瑞奇說，"Let's go down to my place…"，想必這位從城市來的鼠先生要在心裡 OS 一番：「天啊！還要往下走？！難不成他住在地窖裡？」這時候，far 和 down 這兩個字讀起來就很有 fu 了！所以，除了介系詞 in、on、at… 之外，表示「位置」的字還有下面這些喔！

親子英文共讀筆記欄

可以把不熟悉的
單字片語寫在這邊喔!

穿靴子的貓

精選句型	It's one's turn to-V
	Let me + V / Let's + V
	How much...?
片語解析	No Way!
文法解析	冠詞

Puss in Boots

Gad and Sarah were on their sweet
「度假」(on holidays / on vacation) 的概念！用介系詞 on

honeymoon, and they felt carefree in

their fancy castle hotel. But, when

Gad opened the fridge and looked into it, he shouted,
這是 refrigerator 的「簡寫」

"Honey, it's empty! I'm starving." Sarah replied, "So,

it's your turn to buy something back."

"Honey, aren't you going with me?" Gad asked.
這是從 are you not going... 縮寫來的

"No way! I'm so tired. Why not go with Puss? I think
詢問意見，或提出建議，除了 What/How about...? 也可以用 Why not...? 喔
he can help you!" Sarah answered lazily.

Pause & Answer 動動腦

1. Where did Gad and Sarah live on their honeymoon?
（迦得和莎拉去度蜜月時住在哪裡？）

解答在 P.226

穿靴子的貓

　　迦得和莎拉在度蜜月，而且他們在自己的那座精緻的城堡旅館中感到非常優閒。不過，當迦得打開冰箱往裡面看時，他大叫著，「親愛的，冰箱是空的，我好餓呢！」莎拉回答他說，「那麼，輪到你去買些東西回來了吧！」

　　迦得又問：「寶貝，你不跟我一起去嗎？」

　　莎拉懶洋洋地回答：「門都沒有，我好累，為什麼不找小普一起去？我想他應該能幫你的。」

Keywords 關鍵字詞

1	sweet	[swit]	adj.	甜的，甜蜜的
2	honeymoon	[`hʌnɪ͵mun]	n.	蜜月（旅行）
3	carefree	[`kɛr͵fri]	adj.	無憂無慮的
4	fancy	[`fænsɪ]	adj.	精美的，別緻的
5	castle	[`kæsl̩]	n.	城堡
6	fridge	[frɪdʒ]	n.	冰箱
7	empty	[`ɛmptɪ]	adj.	空的
8	starve	[starv]	v.	餓的
9	tired	[taɪrd]	adj.	累的

castle

empty

starve

充　電　站

「貓」的英文，大家都知道是 cat。至於標題的 puss 這個字是「貓咪」，已有「可愛」的意思。另外 kitten 是「小貓咪」，聽過 Hello Kitty 吧？kitty 就是從 kitten 這個字來的喔！另外要說的是 boot（靴子）這個字。靴子當然是鞋子 (shoes) 的一種，只要表示穿在腳上，那一定要加 -s 喔！至於 in boots（穿著靴子的）又為什麼要用 in，而不用 on 呢？那就想想前一單元的 put... in one's shoes 這個片語，大家是不是覺得靈光一閃了呢？

"By the way, don't forget to buy some food ingredients and daily necessities. Take a look at the

等於 every day 的意思，不過它是形容詞，要放在名詞前面喔

list. I wrote them down on it." she added.

So, Gad and Puss once again started their adventure.

等於 every day 的意思，不過它是形容詞，要放在名詞前面喔

This time, they went shopping nearby. "What's on the list, master?" Puss asked.

"Let me check it out... Wow! It's a long list!" Gad

check out 比起 look at、watch等表示
「看看」的動作，有「看個究竟」之意

replied.

"Then we'd better do it separately," Puss suggested.

這是 we had 而不是 we would 的縮寫喔

"That's a good idea. Let's go." Gad said.

Pause & Answer 動動腦

2. What did they go to buy?
（他們要去買什麼？）

解答在 P.226

然後她又說：「對了！別忘記買一些食材和日常用品。看一下這清單。我都已經寫在上面了。」

　　所以迦得跟小普再度踏上他們的冒險旅途，這次他們是到附近購物。

　　小普問說：「主人，清單上寫些什麼呢？」

　　迦得回答說：「我來瞧一瞧…哇！一堆東西。」

　　小普建議說：「那我們最好分頭進行吧！。」

　　迦得說：「這主意不錯！那我們走吧！」

Keywords 關鍵字詞

10	ingredient	[ɪn`grɪdɪənt]	n.	成分；（食物）的原料
11	daily	[`delɪ]	adj.	每日的
12	necessity	[nə`sɛsətɪ]	n.	必需品
13	list	[lɪst]	n.	列表
14	adventure	[əd`vɛntʃə]	n.	冒險
15	nearby	[`nɪr͵baɪ]	adv.	附近
16	master	[`mæstə]	n.	主人
17	separately	[`sɛpərɪtlɪ]	adv.	分開地

food ingredients

master

separate

充　電　站

check 本來是「檢查」的意思，不只是「看看」而已。那麼這邊的 check it out（探個究竟）應該就不難理解了吧！大家一定還聽過什麼 check in、check out 之類的說法，其實都具有相同的本意。比方說，到了機場，準備登機前，我們要先到指定櫃台 check in，領取登機卡及托運行李，到了飯店住宿也是一樣要 check in，然後離開飯店要 check out，都是要核對證件與資料，不是稍微看看而已。

Then Gad handled the food ingredients while Puss

the daily necessities. About an hour later, they met at

連接詞while前後用的是同一個動詞handle，所以Puss後面省略掉這個動詞

the checkout. "Next please," the cashier said.

也可以說 checkout counter 或是 cash desk

"Here we are. How much?" Gad said.

"Just a moment, please; that comes to fifty-five

「合計是…」，「總共是…」的意思，這邊的to後面要接N或Ving喔

dollars exactly!" the cashier answered politely.

"Oh, that's not too bad. I guess it would be more than

that." Gad said.

"Coz I am the member here... Oops! Where's my

這是 Because (因為) 的簡寫，常用於口語中

wallet?"

Pause & Answer 動動腦

3. Did Gad think they need to pay much? Why?

（迦得認為他們得付很多錢嗎？為什麼？）

解答在 P.226

然後迦得負責食材的部分而小普則負責日用品，大約一個小時後，他們在收銀台碰頭。收銀員說：「下一位。」

　　迦得說：「這些是我們的！一共多少錢？」

　　收銀員有禮貌地回答：「請稍等……總共是五十五元整。」

　　迦得說：「哦！那還好，我原以為會更多錢呢！

　　因為我是這裡的會員呀 ... 糟糕！我的錢包呢？」

Keywords 關鍵字詞

18	handle	[`hændl]	v.	處理
19	while	[hwaɪl]	conj.	當…，而…
20	checkout	[`tʃɛkˌaʊt]	n.	收銀台
21	cashier	[kæ`ʃɪr]	n.	收銀員
22	exactly	[ɪg`zæktlɪ]	adv.	精確地
23	politely	[pə`laɪtlɪ]	adv.	有禮貌地
24	guess	[gɛs]	v.	猜想
25	member	[`mɛmbɚ]	n.	會員
26	wallet	[`walɪt]	n.	皮包

cashier

polite

充　電　站

請對方「稍等一下」，在日常生活中，無論是在電話中（on the phone），或到麥當勞、早餐店等，都會聽到店員說出這句話：Just a moment, please = a / one moment, please.（請稍等一下）、Just/Wait a minute（等一下）、Hold on, please（請等一下 — 用於電話中）、Please hold the line. / Don't hang up, please.（請別掛斷電話）。

Useful Expressions 精選句型

It's one's turn to-V 輪到某人…

→ Finally! It's my turn to take a picture with my idol.
終於！輪到我和我的偶像照一張了。

Let me + 原形V 讓我來做…

→ Let me teach you something, and you must listen carefully.
讓我來教你們一些事，你們要認真聽。

How much...? …有多少…？

→ How much exercise do you need for a week?
你一個星期需要多少運動量？

● turn 本來是「翻轉」、「輪動」，所以也可以引申為「輪流的一次機會」。比方說，They take turns to take care of the baby.（他們輪流照顧這個嬰兒。）另外，當大家都在排隊，但卻有人想插隊時，你也可以說 "You have to wait your turn like everyone else here."（你得像這邊每個人一樣，排隊等待。）

● let（讓）在文法上被稱為「使役動詞」，而這種動詞後面接了受詞之後，必須再接「原形動詞」。此外，let 後面如果接 us（we 的受格），可以寫成 Let's，像是 Let's go! 或 Let's do it together.

● How much? 經常用在問「多少錢」，它是 How much is it? 的簡化說法。除了可以用來詢問價錢外，也能用來詢問不可數名詞的量，像是 How much time / How long do you want me to wait?（你要讓我等多久？）可數名詞的話，則可以用 How many...?

片語解析

No way!

● 「沒路！」還是「沒方法！」呢？

way 是相當常見的一個字，它可以表示「路」，但是比起 road（道路，馬路）這個字，它比較常用於「抽象意義」的路，也就是「途徑」或「方法」的意思喔！我們來看看以下三個句子如何表示 way 這個字吧！

A: Please help me.
B: No way. Just do it yourself.

　　No way 其實就等於 No，只是拒絕得更加「狠心」了點

A：請幫幫我。　B：不行。還是自己來！

　　字面是「這條路」，但是
　　中文這樣講很奇怪吧！

Just follow me. This way!
See, do they look great?
跟我來吧！這邊請。看，它們
看起來不賴吧？

Where are we now?
Are we on the wrong way?

　　通常就是指「走反方向了」的意思

我們現在到哪裡了？我們是不是走錯路了？

冠詞的用法

童話故事的結尾無論有多幸福美滿，在現實生活中，冰箱裡的食物還是會吃光，日用品還是需要補貨，所以這邊的小普和迦得不是要去打倒住在城堡裡的魔王，而是…超市的收銀員？也沒這麼誇張啦！就算是擊敗魔王的迦得和小普也要乖乖帶著清單，不然買錯東西回家可是會挨莎拉公主一頓臭罵。我們就來幫忙檢查一下他們買的東西吧！以下就是莎拉給的那張清單：

	ingredients for hamburger		daily necessities
☑	**a** few slices of beef（幾片牛肉）	☑	rolls of **toilet paper**（幾捲衛生紙）
☑	**a** dozen of eggs（一打蛋）	☑	**the** Tide washing powder（Tide 牌洗衣粉）
☑	**an** onion（一顆洋蔥）	☑	**shampoo** 洗髮精
☑	butter（奶油）	☑	hair conditioner（護髮乳）
☑	ground ginger（薑粉）	☑	shower gel（沐浴乳）
☑	**the** dry fish for Puss（Puss 要吃的魚乾）	☐	body lotion（乳液）

哎呀呀…迦得除了忘記帶錢包（後來是小普幫他墊錢），會員卡也在裡面（依然是靠小普），就連莎拉公主要用的乳液都忘了，他回去以後就要倒大楣了……咦！這清單上好像有被動手腳？沒錯！這又是老把戲了，來猜猜看，這些紅色的字又要帶給大家什麼啟示？

大多數的情況下，英文名詞前面需要加上冠詞，冠詞本身分為定冠詞 **the** 和不定冠詞 **a/an**。顧名思義，定冠詞就是有指定，不定冠詞就是沒有指定，而這兩者的差別到底是在哪裡？就以洗髮精 shampoo 為例好了，a shampoo 沒有指定，所以大瓶小瓶，隨便哪一種都可以，但要是寫 the shampoo，那麻煩可大了，加上 the 就代表有所指定，但是光寫 the shampoo 誰知道我們是要哪一瓶，除非說 the shampoo that snow white uses（白雪公主用的那一種）。這樣我們就知道定冠詞和不定冠詞差很多了。

接下來還有一個需要注意的地方是，不定冠詞後面的名詞，字首的「發音」是母音時，為了發音的便利，不定冠詞要從 a 變成 an，請注意！RK 老師是說發音哦！馬上舉個例子：

u 開頭，所以要用 an 嗎？還是檢查一下發音比較妥當！

所以要用 a

university ﹝ˌjunəˋvɚsətɪ﹞ → a university

果然有詐！開頭發音是子音

老師的心機真重……

hour ﹝aʊr﹞ → an hour　所以要用 an

這次是 h 開頭，應該沒問題了吧！不過還是小心為妙。

另外，在某些情況下，名詞前面是不加冠詞的，簡單來說，當名詞是用來「統稱」的時候不加。那什麼是「統稱」？以 butter（奶油）為例，butter 本身不可數，這邊的奶油也沒有特別指定是哪一家或哪個牌子的奶油，而是用來統稱所有的奶油，所以前面不用加冠詞。

各種鞋子的英文

　　我們在前面已經提到過，原來穿鞋子的「穿」，只要用 in 就搞定了，但是別忘了鞋子的單位是什麼？一定要記得加 -s 喔！那麼，我們一起來為這隻「穿靴子」的智慧貓咪，再挑幾雙漂亮的鞋子吧！

(1) leather shoes	皮鞋	(2) slippers	拖鞋	(3) flip-flops	夾腳拖鞋
(4) sandals	涼鞋	(5) rain boots	雨靴	(6) loafers	休閒鞋
(7) high heels	高跟鞋	(8) high-top shoes	高筒鞋	(9) sneakers	運動鞋
(10) tall boots	長靴	※註：「～雙鞋子」可以用「數字 + pair(s) of + 鞋子-s」來表示			

親子英文共讀筆記欄

可以把不熟悉的
單字片語寫在這邊喔！

Unit 10
不萊梅的音樂家

精選句型	S+ be as + adj. + as...
	What about + N / Ving
	see if + S + V...
片語解析	take your time
文法解析	不定代名詞

MP3★Track10

Town Musicians of Bremen

After the Bremen band finally drove

這是drive的過去式，它還可以當「開車」的意思喔

the bad guys away, they worked

together to clean the dirty house and move in. They

decided that: Donkey wiped the windows; Cat swept

and mopped the bedrooms; Dog cooked the dinner.

Rooster was as busy as them, because he had to do

也可以表示「狂妄自大」的人   have to 的過去式，相當於 must 的意思

everything else. "Let's take action!" Rooster

announced loudly. He moved around the house to

oversee the others. Firstly, he went to check Cat.

有冠詞the就是「有指定」，還記得嗎？就是指「不萊梅」這一團的其它三隻動物

Pause & Answer 動動腦

1. Who looks like the leader of the band?

（誰看起來像是這樂團的領導？）

解答在 P.226

不來梅的音樂家

　　不來梅樂團終於將壞人趕走之後，他們一起合力把這髒屋子打掃乾淨然後住進來。他們決定：阿驢擦窗戶；阿貓掃、拖房間的地；阿狗準備晚餐。阿雞和他們一樣忙碌，因為他要負責其他全部的事。

　　「我們開始行動吧！」阿雞大聲宣布。 他穿梭在房子四處監督其他人。首先，他去看看阿貓做得如何。

Keywords 關鍵字詞

1	band	[bænd]	n.	樂團
2	drive away	[draɪv] [əˋwe]	v.	趕走
3	dirty	[ˋdɝtɪ]	adj.	骯髒的
4	wipe	[waɪp]	v.	擦拭；塗抹
5	sweep	[swip]	v.	掃，掃過
6	mop	[mɑp]	v.	用拖把拖洗
7	take action	[tek] [ˋækʃən]	v.	採取行動
8	announce	[əˋnaʊns]	v.	宣布
9	oversee	[ˋovɚˋsi]	v.	監督

drive away

wipe

oversee

　　英文裡的動物名稱，常常都還有分公的、母的、小的…。當然，「雞」也不例外。還記得我們在第一單元那傳叫祖逖起床的Mr. Cock嗎？沒錯，cock和這邊的rooster都是「公雞」的意思，但rooster比cock更為正式，所以「雞年」一般都說 Year of Rooster，而不是 Year of Cock。那麼「母雞」的英文呢？是hen這個字喔！至於最常見的chick（複數chicken）則多指「小雞」。

143

"Hey Cat, how's everything going?" Rooster asked

這邊的 going 有點像第八課提到過的 How's going? 中的 going，都有問候之意

curiously. "I cleaned four bedrooms, and some small

ones." Cat answered as she mopped the floor.

Then, Rooster went upstairs to see Donkey. "Hey

「樓上」的意思，那麼樓下就是 downstairs

Donkey, are things OK with you?" Rooster asked

breathlessly. "See? All the glass on the first and

breath (呼吸) + less (否定) → 沒了呼吸不就要掛了？沒這麼嚴重啦！就是指「喘得快透不過氣來」而已

second floors looks so shiny!" Donkey replied

知道 look 為什麼用第三人稱單數嗎？注意看一下主詞是誰？是 glass 喔！

proudly. "But... what about the bookcases?" Rooster

pointed to them. "Oops! I didn't do any! I'll do it

later." Donkey said.

"OK. There's no hurry. But don't forget to pick up the

也可以簡單說 "No hurry!" 就可以了，相反地，要叫人家快一點時，可以說 Hurry up!

garbage there." Rooster said.

Pause & Answer 動動腦

2. Who was working on the second floor?

（在二樓工作的是誰？）

解答在 P.226

阿雞好奇地問：「嗨，阿貓！一切順利吧？」阿貓一邊拖地一邊回答：「我已經掃好四間臥房，還有幾間小的。」

　　接著，阿雞上樓去看看阿驢。阿雞氣喘吁吁問著：「嗨，阿驢，你這邊還好吧？」阿驢驕傲地回答說，「看到沒？一、二樓所有玻璃都看起來亮晶晶呢！」

　　阿雞指著書櫃問：「不過……那些書櫃呢？」阿驢回答：「糟！我一個都還沒弄！我待會兒就擦。」

　　阿雞說：「好的。不急！不過別忘了那邊的垃圾要撿起來喔！」

Keywords 關鍵字詞

10	floor	[flor]	n.	地板；樓層
11	upstairs	[ˌʌpˋstɛrz]	adv.	往樓上
12	breathlessly	[ˋbrɛθləslɪ]	adv.	喘吁吁地
13	glass	[glæs]	n.	玻璃
14	shiny	[ˋʃaɪnɪ]	adj.	閃亮的
15	bookcase	[ˋbʊkˌkes]	n.	書櫃
16	point	[pɔɪnt]	v.	指向（＋ to）；指出（＋ out）
17	pick up	[ˋpɪkʌp]	v.	撿起
18	garbage	[ˋgɑrbɪdʒ]	n.	垃圾

充電站

glass 在故事中是「玻璃」的意思。我們知道，「玻璃」是不可數名詞，如果要用數量表現的話，可以說 a piece of glass（一片玻璃）。不過，它如果當「玻璃杯」時，就變成可數名詞了，比如說 two glasses of wine（兩杯酒）。另外，「眼鏡」的英文是 glasses，因為眼鏡本來就有兩塊鏡片，就像前面學過的 shoes（鞋子）一樣，都是以複數型態出現的喔！

Then, he went to the kitchen to see if the dinner was ready. "Wow! It smells good." Rooster said. "Thanks!

smell 是「感官動詞」之一，後面要接形容詞

The kitchen was just a disaster. I need some time to

它是「災難」的意思，用在這邊來表示「一團亂」，比 mess 這個字「亂」的程度更嚴重

clean it up before we can enjoy the dinner." Dog answered. "OK! Just take your time. Everybody is still busy with their chores." Rooster said.

be busy with + 事情 → 表示「忙著某件事情」，如果要表示忙著「做某件事情」，要變成 be busy (in) + Ving

The whole afternoon's effort made everyone so tired.

After enjoying the long-awaited dinner, they lounged

這是個複合形容詞，字面上應該不難理解吧！
表示「等候已久的」

on the sofa, when...

"Hey you! What's the smell? What are you COOKING? Dog!" Rooster shouted!

Pause & Answer 動動腦

3. How did these band members feel after dinner?
（這樂團成員們在晚餐過後感覺如何？）

解答在 P.226

然後，他到廚房去看看晚餐好了沒。

「哇！好香喔！」阿雞說。

「謝謝！廚房剛才真是一團亂，我需要些時間清理一下，我們才能享用晚餐喔！」阿狗回答。阿雞說：「好吧，慢慢來。大家也還在忙著他們的雜務。」

一整個下午的辛勞讓大家感到無比疲累。在享用了等候多時的晚餐之後，他們悠閒地在沙發上休息。這時候 ...

「喂，大家！那什麼味道？阿狗，你還在煮什麼東西啊？」阿雞大叫著。

Keywords 關鍵字詞

19	kitchen	[ˋkɪtʃɪn]	n.	廚房
20	smell	[smɛl]	v./n.	聞起來；味道
21	disaster	[dɪˋzæstɚ]	n.	災難
22	chore	[tʃor]	n.	家庭雜務
23	whole	[hol]	adj.	整個的
24	effort	[ˋɛfɚt]	n.	努力
25	tired	[taɪrd]	adj.	疲累的
26	lounge	[laʊndʒ]	v.	（懶洋洋地）倚，靠

disaster

tired

充電站

這段出現了「廚房」（kitchen）這個字，那就順便來學學家裡面各「區域」（area）的英文吧：客廳（living room）、飯廳（dining room）、臥室（bedroom）、主臥（master bedroom）、客房（guest room）、浴室（bathroom）、廁所（toilet）、儲藏室（storage room）、更衣室（walk-in closet）、夾層樓（mezzanine [ˋmɛzəˏnin]）。

Useful Expressions 精選句型

(speech bubbles: You did a great job! / 太棒了!)

S+ be as + adj. + as… 和…一樣…

→ Peter's performance is as good as Jenny's.

基於「對等關係」，這邊可不能用 as good as Jenny 喔

彼得的演出和 Jenny 的一樣棒。

What about + N/Ving 要不然…如何？

(speech bubbles: What about you? / We have no idea!)

→ What about taking action right now?

What about 後面如果接「人」的話，表示
「詢問對方的意見」
現在就展開行動，如何？

see if + S + V… 看看是否…？

→ The kids stretched their heads from the window to see if the bad

這邊的 stretch 用法和 Unit 1 的有點不同喔！

guys were already gone. 不是「伸懶腰」，而是「把…伸出」的意思

孩子們從窗戶伸出頭來看看那些壞人是不是走了。

Wow!

148

Sentence Patterns 句型解析

- as...as... (和 ... 一樣 ...) 是「同等比較」的常用句型,它最基本的句型就是 as + 原級 (形容詞 / 副詞)+ as...。比如說 He can dance as well as Jenny (can). (他跳舞可以跳得和 Jenny 一樣好。)另外,第一個 as 也可以用 so 來取代喔!比如說:I don't run so fast as my sister (does). (我跑的沒有姊姊快。)

- 除了 what about 之外,how about 也很常用,事實上,兩者幾乎沒有什麼差別,都可以用來表示「提出建議」、「詢問意見」。但有一點必須注意的是,how about 後面是可以接一個句子的,但 what about 沒有這種用法。比如說:How about we take a walk along the beach? (我們到海灘去走走如何?)

- see 原本是「看見」的意思,它跟 look 主要差別在「有沒有認真看」。如果只是「看看」就忘了或不在意什麼,那就是 look 的意思。所以,「see if + 子句」這個句型有「用眼睛去確認」一件事之意。我們來看看下面這句中文怎麼翻:

Dad: Wow! You're as sweet as honey today.

Mom: Your words are, too. But I need to see if there's something wrong with you today!

解答在 P.226

take your time

● 什麼叫「拿你的時間」呢？

take your time 其實也就是這一課另一個片語 "No hurry!" 或 "No rush!"（不急，慢慢來！）的意思。take 這個動詞如果和 time 搭配使用的話，就會解釋成「花費」，比如說：It took me three hours to finish the job.（我花了 3 小時完成這工作）。下面我們就來看看 take 還可以怎麼用吧！

There's no hurry. Please just take your time to set the table.
不急。您可以慢慢擺設餐桌。

I was taken by surprise

不要只會 I'm so surprised!，學學用 I was taken by surprise… 來表示「對…感到驚訝」吧！

with my birthday gift.
我對於我的生日禮物感到無比驚訝。

How come I'm always late for school? I

How come + 子句？ 表示「怎麼會…？」

really need to take action to keep early

再複習一下第一段出現的這個片語吧！

hours.
我怎麼老是上學遲到？我真的得採取行動，早睡早起才行。

不定代名詞

我們這篇故事源自於《不來梅樂團》…這一次他們的新任務是大掃除，於是大家各司其職，而公雞也很盡責地巡視大家的進度。這時候就出現了一個有趣的問題。我們先來看看下面兩個句子：

I cleaned four bedrooms, and some small **ones**.

Oops! I didn't do **any**!

又要再動動腦了！這兩個字為什麼變成紅色？我們把上面的句子動個手腳，再看清楚一下點：

I cleaned four bedrooms, and some small **bedrooms**.

Oops! I didn't do **any bookcases**!

注意到了嗎？句子紅色的部分都變得比較長。如果使用之前那幾個字來代替，意思不但完全沒有改變，而且更加簡單通順，我們何樂而不為？而最上面兩個句子裡的紅字，正是這個單元的文法主題：不定代名詞。

代名詞大概可以細分成九個種類，而不定代名詞正是其中一種，之所以會被冠上「不定」之名，是因為它不是用來指特定對象，比如説：I've cleaned four bedrooms and some small **ones**，我們沒有辦法從句中得知 ones 所指的是哪幾間小的。同理，我們仍然沒有辦法知道 I haven't done **any** yet 中的 any 所指的是哪一個（驢子的意思是，所有書櫃的玻璃都還沒擦），那如果把這些句子都加入指示代名詞會變成怎麼樣呢？

"I've cleaned four bedrooms and **these** small ones."

"…I haven't done **those** yet…"

其實我們將故事中的句子換成上面這幾句都沒有問題，不過條件是公雞能夠看見這些、那些房間、窗戶等東西的前提下，否則他怎麼知道是指哪些東西？

其他常用的不定代名詞還有以下這些，老師順便附上一些諺語讓大家更加深印象：

one	Two heads are better than one.	三個臭皮匠勝過一個諸葛亮。
none	A man of all trades is master of none.	樣樣通，樣樣鬆。
all	All is well that ends well.	皆大歡喜（只要結局是好的就好了）。
another	When one door shuts, another opens.	天無絕人之路。

各種樓梯的英文

　　原來不來梅樂團們的新家是一棟大別墅，裡面有好幾層樓呢！害得阿雞老大巡視大家工作狀況時，還得爬上爬下（upstairs and downstairs）。所以為了讓老大下次可以不必再搞得喘吁吁地（breathlessly），我們來幫他們加裝樓梯吧！下面有五種樓梯或梯子，大家來猜看看他們的英文怎麼說吧！

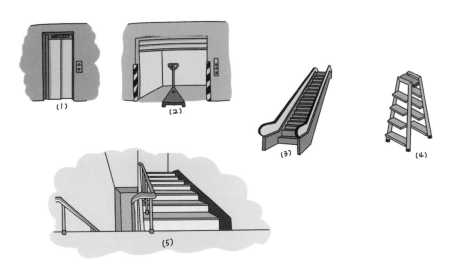

(1) elevator	電梯	(2) cargo lift	貨梯	(3) escalator	手扶梯
(4) ladder	梯子	(5) staircase	樓梯間		

親子英文共讀筆記欄

可以把不熟悉的
單字片語寫在這邊喔！

Unit 11
識途老馬

精選句型 S + can't remember + 子句

tell sb + 子句

Are you sure (that) + 子句

about / of + 名詞

片語解析 watch your step

文法解析 動狀詞

Watch your language!

Unit 11

The Old Horse Knows the Way

"Where are we? I don't want to get lost in this scary place."

"Don't worry, my lord; we're almost there."

be here或be there表示「到了這裡／那裡」

King Chi-Hsuan traveled a long way in spring for a fight. When the war ended, it was already winter. The land was covered with snow. So, the king couldn't

表示「被…覆蓋」。英文裡表示「滿」都會用到 with，比如 be filled with… (充滿著…)

remember which road he took. "Oh, dear god, I remembered crossing a river. If I get there, I will

這是本單元的文法重點喔！

know the way home." Chi-Hsuan cried to the sky.

way + 地方副詞 → 往…的路

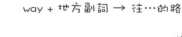

Pause & Answer 動動腦

1 Why did they get lost?
    （他們為什麼迷路了？）

解答在 P.226

156

識途老馬

「這裡是哪裡？我可不想在這鬼地方迷路啊！」

「別擔心陛下，我們就快到了。」

齊宣王在春天時長途跋涉去抗敵，而當戰事結束時，已經是冬天了。大地被白雪覆蓋。所以他已記不得走過的路了。

齊宣王對著天空哭喊著：「噢，天哪！我記得跨過了一條河啊，要是我能夠到那邊，就能知道回家的路了。」

Keywords 關鍵字詞

1	get lost	[gɛt] [lɔst]	v.	迷路
2	scary	[`skɛrɪ]	adj.	可怕的
3	worry	[`wɝɪ]	v.	擔心
4	almost	[`ɔl‚most]	adv.	幾乎
5	travel	[`trævl̩]	v.	旅行
6	fight	[faɪt]	n.	打鬥
7	cover	[`kʌvɚ]	v.	覆蓋
8	cross	[krɔs]	v.	越過，穿過

get lost

cover

cross

所謂一年四季（four seasons in a year）的春夏秋冬，英文的說法分別是 spring、summer、fall / autumn、winter。不過 spring 這個字還有「泉」的意思，比如 hot spring（溫泉）、cold spring（冷泉），而 fall 還有「掉落」的意思，大家可以想像葉子很容易掉落的季節，就是秋季了。而全部掉光光就是「all 脫」，很像 autumn 這個字的發音吧！

"I can tell you, my lord." the old horse, Gyan, said.

"Why didn't you let me know earlier?" Chi-Hsuan

early 的副詞比較級，表示「更早一點」

thundered.

這個字原本是「打雷」的意思，所以當作「喊叫」時，比shout、yell 更大聲喔

"Because you never asked me, my lord." Gyan

answered.

"Anyway, now tell me how I can see a river." Chi-

Hsuan asked.

這是個介系詞，表示「往⋯方向」，常與walk、
run、go⋯這些「前進」的字眼搭配使用

"Um, just go straight toward the east and there is a

valley. Walk along the valley. When you see a pond,

turn right. Then, keep going through the woods and

keep + Ving表示「一直／持續做某事」

go all the way to the end and you will see a river."

Gyan said patiently.

Pause & Answer 動動腦

2. Where is the pond?

（池塘在哪裡？）

解答在 P.226

老馬賈恩說：「陛下，我可以告訴您。」

齊宣王大聲咆嘯地說：「那你怎麼不早點讓我知道？」

賈恩回答：「因為陛下您從來沒問過我啊！」

齊宣王問：「反正，現在就告訴我，怎樣才能看到一條河呢？」

賈恩有耐心地說：「嗯，就朝著東方一直走，那裡有一座山谷。沿著山谷走，當你看到一個池塘的時候向右轉，然後繼續走，穿過一座森林，一直走到底你就會看到河。」

Keywords 關鍵字詞

9	lord	[lɔrd]	n.	陛下，君主
10	thunder	[ˋθʌndɚ]	v.	大聲咆嘯
11	anyway	[ˋɛnɪˏwe]	adv.	無論如何，反正
12	**straight**	[stret]	adv.	直接地
13	**valley**	[ˋvælɪ]	n.	山谷
14	**pond**	[pand]	n.	池塘
15	**woods**	[wʊdz]	n.	樹林
16	all the way		adv.	一直

thunder

valley

pond

充 電 站

英文裡的「方位」（direction），就是以「東南西北」為基準，分別是 east、south、west、north，我們常常在地圖上看到大寫字母 E、S、W、N 代表的就是四個方位。另外，如果要表示「東南」，英文的說法是 southeast，要把「南」放在「東」前面喔！所以「西北」的英文就是 northwest。另外，如果要表示形容詞的「東（方）的」、「南（方）的」、「東南（方）的」…等，要加字尾 -ern 喔！它們的英文分別是 eastern、southern、southeastern…等。

159

So, Chi-Hsuan followed Gyan's directions and finally arrived at the place Gyan mentioned, but there

arrive at + 小地方、arrive in + 大地方

wasn't any river.

"WHERE IS THE RIVER!" Chi-Hsuan yelled again and stamped on the ground.

"Watch your step, my lord. We are right in the middle of it!" Gyan warned.

這邊不是當「對的」、「正確的」，也不是「右邊」意思，而是指「正好」、「恰巧」

這是第四單元學過的 there be…（有…）句型的延伸喔！

"Since we are here, there should be a mountain in the north, but I don't see any mountain! Are you sure we are at THE river." Chi-Hsuan asked.

"Sorry my lord, but you just said A river." Gyan

還記得前面學過I'm sorry but…這個句型嗎？

chuckled softly.

Pause & Answer 動動腦

3. What did Chi-Hsuan want to see at last?
   （齊宣王最後想看到什麼？）

解答在 P.226

於是，齊宣王就依照著賈恩的指示，最後到達了賈恩提到的那個地方，但是那邊並沒有什麼河流。

　　齊宣王再次暴跳如雷地說：「說好的河呢？」說完還大力的踱著腳。

　　賈恩警告說：「陛下請小心，我現在在正在它的正中央。」

　　齊宣王問：「既然我們已經到了，北邊應該有座山才對啊！但是我怎麼連個鬼影子都沒看見？你確定我們現在是在『那』條河上嗎。」

　　「抱歉陛下！」賈恩溫柔地偷笑著，「您剛是說『一條』河吧！」

Keywords 關鍵字詞

17	direction	[dəˋrɛkʃən]	n.	指示，方向
18	arrive	[əˋraɪv]	v.	抵達
19	mention	[ˋmɛnʃən]	v.	提及
20	stamp	[stæmp]	v.	跺腳；踩踏
21	ground	[graʊnd]	n.	地面
22	middle	[ˋmɪd!]	n.	中間
23	mountain	[ˋmaʊntn]	n.	山
24	chuckle	[ˋtʃʌk!]	v.	偷笑
25	softly	[ˋsɔftlɪ]	adv.	溫柔地

direction

chuckle

在英文裡，表示「河流」、「溪流」的英文，主要有 river、stream 和 brook 這三個字。以「大小條」作區分的話，就是 river > stream > brook 了。比如，「淡水河」（Tamshui River）、「大漢溪」（Dahan River），而 stream 這個字比較不出現在地名上，像是河川的「上游」（upstream）、「下游」（downstream）會用到這個字。而 brook 通常指「小溪流」。

Useful Expressions 精選句型

S + can't remember + 子句 無法記得⋯

→ Mom can't remember where her glasses are.
媽咪不記得她的眼鏡放在哪了。

tell sb + 子句 告訴某人⋯

→ Could you tell me how you planned to lose weight?
可以請你告訴我，你是怎麼減肥的嗎？ 「減肥」也可以說成
reduce weight 喔！

Are you sure (that) +子句   你確定⋯？
about / of + 名詞

→ Are you sure you guys are ready to fight?

很常見的組合詞，表示「你們各位⋯」、「大家⋯」

你確定你們大家已經準備好上場格鬥了嗎？

162

● 當我們要問人家，「我的眼鏡呢？」英文可以說 Where **are** my glass**es**？ 或是 Where is **my pair of** glasses?（我那副的眼鏡呢？）這樣的問句，我們稱之為「直接問句」。但是大家有注意到嗎？這邊 where 後面的名詞和 be 動詞位置卻是肯定句的擺放方式！這就是文法中所謂的「間接問句」（沒錯！這邊第二個句型也是）。千萬別寫成 I can't remember where are my glasses. 喔！

● 英文裡，表示「說」的英文，最基本的有 **say**、**speak**、**tell** 這三個字。大家知道「說故事」、「說英文」、「說話」的「說」，分別要用哪個字嗎？來，跟著老師一起念：**Say** something, please!（請說說話吧！）、I can **speak** English.（我會說英文。）、Let me **tell** you a love story.（我來跟大家說個愛情故事。）

● 當我們要對別人說的一番話提出疑問或抱持懷疑態度時，"Are you sure?"（你確定嗎？）是很常見的用語。其實它後面還以可以接一個「子句」，包括 **that** 開頭的，或是 **wh- / if** 開頭的皆可。此外，如果是 that 子句，that 是可以省略的喔！最後，我們來看看下面這句中文怎麼翻吧：

A：請告訴我，未來我是不是會變有錢人？

B：我很確定⋯我沒辦法回答這個問題喔！

解答在 P.226

片語解析

watch your step

- 什麼叫「看著你的步伐」呢？

watch 這個動詞，除了可以用來表示「看」電視、「看」電影，它也可以當名詞用，最基本的就是「手錶」的意思，所以大家可以想想，我們為什麼要「看錶」？是不是有「注意」時間的意味在內？所以囉！watch 這個字也常被用來表示「留意」、「小心注意」的意思。以下我們就來看看 watch 如何表現「留意」吧！

Watch your step!

You should watch your step when going downstairs.
下樓梯時要注意台階。

Watch your back!

Trust me! I'll watch your back.
相信我！我會罩你的。

Watch your language!

Watch your language! Don't say four letter words.

英文的「三字經」是 four letter words，letter 是「字母」的意思，所以大家知道是指哪個字了嗎？
注意你的言詞！別罵三字經。

164

動狀詞

大家還記得在《穿長靴的貓》那一課的文法重點─冠詞的用法嗎？所以，要是齊宣王當初是說 "Anyway, now tell me how can I see the river?"，那麼買恩應該不會誤會了吧？也很難說，其實搞不好牠根本是故意抓齊宣王的語病，跟他玩了個文字遊戲囉！不管怎樣，齊宣王的記性還是不錯的，因為他說：

I remembered crossing a river.

哎呀！又有紅字了！這邊的crossing又暗藏什麼玄機呢？首先，我們來翻一下這個句子：我記得越過一條河流。

小朋友們，請問一下，這個句子有幾個「動作」？沒錯！有「記得」和「越過」這兩個動作，但是英文的句子有一個很重要、很重要、很重要（因為真的很重要，所以說三次）的原則，那就是：一個句子只能有一個動詞。那麼如果要表示第二、甚至多個「動作」時怎麼辦？

這就是本單元要講的文法重點了 ─ 動狀詞（顧名思義就是「具有動作狀態」詞），又被稱為「準動詞」。以下我們就用表格來介紹一下「動狀詞」吧：

說明 ＼ 動狀詞	不定詞	動名詞	分詞
表現形式	to + V	V-ing	V-ing 或 V-ed
扮演角色	N. / Adj. / Adv.	N.	Adj.

接下來，我們來看看下面幾個句子錯在哪裡：

I don't want get lost in this scary place.
The land covered with snow.
Then, keep go to through the woods.

錯在哪裡，大家看出來了嗎？別偷偷翻到前面去看喔！我們從下面的表格，加上紅色標示，大家就一目了然啦！

錯誤句子	正確句子
I don't want **get lost** in this scary place.	I don't want **to get lost** in this scary place.
The land **covered** with snow.	The land **was covered** with snow.
Then, keep **to go** through the woods.	Then, keep **going** through the woods.

第一個句子出現了兩個動詞吧！want 和 get 怎麼可以擺在一起呢？所以我們必須讓第二個動詞 get 變成「動狀詞」裡的「不定詞」to get。

第二個句子看起來好像沒什麼錯，其實要注意的是 cover 這個動詞的用法喔！因為 land 是「被覆蓋」，所以必須用被動式 be covered with…（被…覆蓋），這邊的 covered 不算是動詞喔！

第三個句子看起來好像也沒什麼問題，但其實 keep 後面如果要接一個動作時，一定要用動名詞，表示「一直／保持…（某個動作的進行）」。

「問路」英文

　　讓我們一邊學著「識途老馬」教我們的 go straight toward…（往…直走）、walk along…（沿著…走）、turn right（向右轉）、go all the way to the end（一直走到底），一邊學學下面這張十字路口圖中的標的物英文名稱吧！

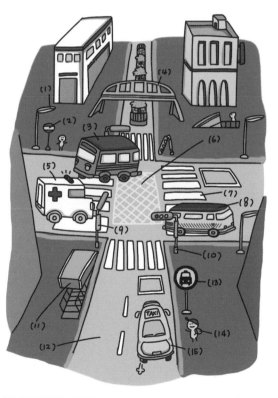

(1)	streetlight 路燈
(2)	bus stop 公車站牌
(3)	bus 公車
(4)	overpass 天橋
(5)	ambulance 救護車
(6)	intersection 十字路口
(7)	crosswalk 斑馬線
(8)	school bus 校車
(9)	street sign 路標

(10) traffic lights 紅綠燈	(11) underpass 地下道	(12) lane 車道
(13) taxi stand 計程車站	(14) pedestrian 行人	(15) taxi / cab 計程車

可以把不熟悉的
單字片語寫在這邊喔！

Unit 12
螞蟻和蟋蟀

精選句型　S+ go to talk to + 人

be busy + Ving

S + had better + 原形 V

片語解析　Tell me about it!

文法解析　動詞過去式

MP3★Track12

The Ants and
the Cricket

It was five o'clock on a freezing

December morning. Palani, a cricket, was

seeking for food with his stomach rumbling; besides,

「介系詞with + N + Ving」表示對於前面句子的「附帶說明」

he felt dying while catching a cold. "Why doesn't he

die 的現在分詞形式，如同 lie (說謊) → lying，tie (繫住) → tying

get some food and clothes?" you might ask. Let me

tell you what happened to this poor creature.

"what happened to + 某人" 表示「某人怎麼了？」

Last summer, when Palani went to enjoy the field

「去年夏天」可別寫成 last year's summer 喔

view near an ant nest, he saw all the ants working

hard. Then he met an ant, Amelie, and had a chat

「聊天」可以用chat或talk喔

with her.

Pause & Answer 動動腦

1 Why did the cricket feel dying?
   （為什麼這隻蟋蟀感覺快死了？）

解答在 P.226

170

螞蟻和蟋蟀

在一個寒冷的十二月凌晨。帕拉尼 ─ 一隻蟋蟀 ─ 正在找尋著食物，牠的肚子咕嚕咕嚕作響著；而且，牠又感冒了，也覺得自己快死了。你或許會問：「為什麼他不去弄點食物和衣服呢？」就讓我來告訴你這可憐傢伙發生了什麼事吧！

去年夏天，當帕拉尼到一處蟻窩附近享受田野風光時，他看見所有的螞蟻都在努力地工作。然後他遇到一隻螞蟻，艾蜜莉，並且和她聊了一下。

 Keywords 關鍵字詞

1	freezing	[`frizɪŋ]	adj.	寒冷的
2	cricket	[`krɪkɪt]	n.	蟋蟀
3	seek	[sik]	v.	找尋
4	rumble	[`rʌmb!]	v.	咕嚕咕嚕叫著
5	dying	[`daɪɪŋ]	adj.	垂死的
6	creature	[`kritʃɚ]	n.	生物
7	ant	[ænt]	n.	螞蟻
8	nest	[nɛst]	n.	巢
9	work hard	[wɝk] [hɑrd]	v.	努力工作

rumble

nest

生病或感冒的時候，只會說 I'm sick. 或 I have a cold. 嗎？要是你喉嚨痛、頭暈、想吐或是拉肚子（前面「鈴鐺貓」那個單元學過喔！）又該怎麼表達呢？我們一次把它學起來吧！喉嚨痛，可以說 I got a sore throat.，頭暈，可以說 I'm feeling dizzy.，想吐的話，是 I feel like throwing up. 那麼，流鼻涕，我們可以說 runny nose。

"It's a nice sunny day, isn't it?" Palani greeted Amelie

joyfully.

這個字的名詞是 joy（喜悅、歡樂）

"Tell me about it! But it might rain this afternoon!"

Amelie answered.

當作「跡象」、「前兆」解時，後面可以接
that子句，而that可省略

"I doubt it! There's no sign it's going to rain. Anyway,

what are you ants busy doing?" Palani wondered

"We are collecting food for the winter! Besides, it's

這邊的it是指winter，不是指「天氣」喔

likely to be freezing." Amelie answered.

"Probably. But it also might be warmer this winter,"

那麼這個it呢？沒錯！它是指the weather

Palani said.

Palani was lucky. It was a bit warm that winter. So, he

planned to take a walk there again.

Pause & Answer 動動腦

2. How's the weather that day when Palani met Amelie?
（帕拉尼見到艾蜜莉的那天，天氣如何？）

解答在 P.226

帕拉尼友善地問候著：「今天真是晴朗的好天氣啊，不是嗎？」

艾蜜莉回答：「可不是嗎！但今天下午可能會下雨！」

「我很懷疑！沒有什麼跡象顯示會下雨啊。對了，妳們螞蟻正在忙些什麼？」帕拉尼對此感到納悶。

艾蜜莉回答：「我們正在收集冬天的食物。而且，到時候可能很冷喔！」

帕拉尼說：「也許吧。不過今年冬天也可能更暖和些呢！」

帕拉尼很幸運，那年冬天還算溫暖，因此他計畫再到那裡去散散步。

Keywords 關鍵字詞

10	sunny	[`sʌnɪ]	adj.	晴朗的
11	joyfully	[`dʒɔɪfəlɪ]	adv.	愉快地
12	doubt	[daʊt]	v.	懷疑
13	sign	[saɪn]	n.	跡象
14	wonder	[`wʌndɚ]	v.	(好奇地) 想知道
15	collect	[kə`lɛkt]	v.	收集，堆積
16	probably	[`prɑbəblɪ]	adv.	可能地
17	take a walk		ph.	散步

wonder

collect

take a walk

平常大家在聊天時，總是會聽到這樣的對話：「你這次考得還不錯，對不對？」、「你也考得很好，不是嗎？」、「你明天會來吧，是不是？」這三個句子裡的「對不對？」、「不是嗎？」、「是不是？」，就是所謂「附加問句」。附加問句和主要子句之間要用逗號分開，就像這一段開頭的 It's a nice sunny day, isn't it?

173

"Hey, It's me again! What a scorching day! Why not

跟What / How about一樣，都可以用來詢問意見，但why not後面要接原形V喔

go swimming with me?" Palani invited Amelie.

"I told you last year, I have to …"

"But last winter was warm! Just take a rest and go

也可以說take a break

out with me!" Palani cut in. "The weather is ever-

changing! It might be freezing this winter! You'd

better collect some food beforehand." Amelie said

seriously and went back to work right away.

記得前面學過的at once（立刻）嗎？

She was right this time, and Palani was chilled and

starved to death later, as suggested at the beginning

前面學過die的現在分詞dying，再學一下它的名詞death吧

of this story.

Pause & Answer 動動腦

3. What did Amelie suggest Palani should do?
（艾蜜莉建議帕拉尼應該做什麼？）

解答在 P.226

「嘿！我又來了。今天真是熱啊！何不跟我去游泳呢？」帕拉尼提出了邀請。

「我去年就跟你說過了，我得……」

帕拉尼打斷她的話說：「但是去年冬天很溫暖啊！你就休息一下，跟我出去玩吧！」艾蜜莉嚴肅地說：「天氣是變化的！今年冬天可能會很冷！你最好還是預先囤積一些食物吧。」說完，她就回去工作了。

這次，她說對了。而帕拉尼後來因為又冷又餓而死了 — 就如同這故事一開始即暗示著。

Keywords 關鍵字詞

18	scorching	[`skɔrtʃɪŋ]	adj.	炎熱的
19	take a rest		ph.	休息一下
20	cut in	[`kʌtɪn]	v.	插話，介入
21	ever-changing	[`ɛvɚ`tʃendʒɪŋ]	adj.	一直在變化的
22	beforehand	[bɪ`for͵hænd]	adv.	預先
23	seriously	[`sɪrɪəslɪ]	adv.	嚴肅地
24	chill	[tʃɪl]	v.	使感到寒冷
25	death	[dɛθ]	n.	死亡
26	suggest	[sə`dʒɛst]	v.	暗示

scorching

cut in

充 電 站

當帕拉尼想約艾蜜莉出去玩時，只見她很嚴肅地 (seriously) 連說三句話，說完頭也不回地就離開了，可惜帕拉尼連心裡面來個 OS：Are you serious?（你是認真的嗎？）都沒有，才會下場淒慘呢！不過這句話其實超好用的，而且很常聽到，有時候，該睡覺了，但小朋友還是在玩不停，這時候爸爸媽媽就會展現威嚴地說：Go to bed right now! I'm serious.（現在馬上去睡覺！我是認真的。）

175

Useful Expressions 精選句型

S (人) + go to + 原形V　去做某事

→ Do you go to tell Daddy about that?

這邊 to 是可以省略的喔！

你去跟爹地講那件事了嗎？

S (人) + be busy + Ving

→ Everybody is busy cleaning the house.

每個人忙著清理屋子。

S (人) + had better + 原形 V　最好是…？

→ We had better arrive there on time before it's too late.

on time 是「準時」，in time 是「及時」

我們最好準時到那裏，不然就太晚了。

176

Sentence Patterns 句型解析

- come、go 這兩個動詞常用在 come / go + to-V 的句型中，就等於 come / go + and + 原形 V。所以課文裡的這句 Palani went to enjoy the field view near an ant nest... 可改成 Palani went and enjoyed ...。不過在現代美式用語中，to 和 and 也經常被省略了。比如說：Come look at this. = Come and look at this. = Come to look at this.

- be busy 除了用於「忙著做什麼事」的句型，也可以用在「忙於什麼事」，後面接介系詞 with，例如 He's busy with his study.（他忙著自己的課業。）

- had better 可以用來表示「提出建議」。此外 had 雖然是 have 的過去式，但是 had better 並沒有「過去」的意思喔！它是個「助動詞」，後面一律接原形動詞。

最後，我們來看看下面這句英文怎麼翻吧：

The angry mother went to talk to his son and said, "You'd better wash your hands first."

解答在 P.226

177

Tell me about it!

● 什麼叫「快告訴我！」？

這句話字面意思是「告訴我怎麼回事！」比方說，What's your plan? **Tell me about it.**（你有什麼計畫？告訴我吧！）不過在這個單元中，蟻妹用這句話，來回答蟋蟀兄的「今天天氣很好，不是嗎？」這可就有意思了！因為這邊的 **Tell me about it!** 其實是有點「反諷」意味，也就是「還用你告訴我啊！」、「那是當然的啊！」的意思。我們再來看看還有什麼類似講法吧！

A: You're such a reliable man!
B: Tell me about it!
A：你是個值得信賴的男人！
B：那當然！

A: You're always a friend in need.
B: You can say that again!
「你可以再說一遍」就是非常認同的意思
A：你一直都是個患難見真情的朋友。B：說得好！

A: Did you hear a fart?
B: You bet! And it's so stinky.
bet 本來是「賭」的意思，所以「你可以賭了」就有「表示肯定」的意味
A：你有聽見放屁的聲音嗎？ B：有啊！而且好臭。

動詞的過去式

中文和英文有個很不一樣的概念，那就是「時態」（tense），它是指所描述的句子中，事件發生的時間背景，可以分成「未來將會發生的事」、「過去發生過的事」、「正在進行中的事」，以及「陳述事實」。

在中文裡，時態通常只需要在前後加上一些修飾的文字，比如用「時間副詞」表示，而動詞本身沒有任何改變。而英文的動詞在「未來」和「陳述事實」時和中文差不多，但是在「過去」和「進行中」這兩個時態可就大不相同了！

I play soccer.	我會踢足球。
I am playing soccer.	我正在踢足球。
I played soccer.	我踢過足球了。
I will play soccer.	我要去踢足球了。

在上面四個句子中，我們可以明顯地發現，英文和中文的現在簡單式及未來簡單式基本上沒有差別，但在現在進行式和過去簡單式中，英文在動詞上就做了些手腳，也就是綠色的部分。而我們這一次的重點就是放在第三句：過去式！

過去式是用來描述「已經發生過的事情」，所以不論是兩億年前（大概是侏儸紀世界吧！）或是兩秒鐘以前，都屬於過去式。而過去式本身又可以再細分成「過去簡單式」、「過去進行式」、「過去完成式」和「過去完成進行式」，不過我們這個單元的主題先放在「過去簡單式」。

179

其實，如果能夠造出「現在簡單式」的句子，那麼「過去簡單式」的句子就只剩下一個地方需要注意了，那就是「動詞變化」。動詞的變化可分為兩種，第一種是規則變化：

直接加ed					answer	→	answered
字尾是…	e	就直接給它加一個d上去			love		loved
	子音 + y		把y變成ied		cry		cried
	母音 + y		直接加ed		play		played
	短母音 +	一個 子音	重複字尾加ed		plan		planned
		兩個 子音	直接加ed		fill		filled

第二種就是不規則變化，雖然有點令人討厭，因為沒有規則可循，但不規則變化的動詞，通常都是些很常見的動詞，比如說：

bring	bought	帶	run	ran	跑	buy	brought	買
break	broke	打破	say	said	說	see	saw	看
do	did	做	sit	sit	做	catch	caught	抓
tell	told	告訴	come	came	來	write	wrote	寫
drink	drank	喝	cut	cut	剪	eat	ate	吃
hit	hit	打	get	got	得到	put	put	放
give	gave	給	go	went	去	have	had	有

不知大家有沒有注意到整個故事的時態。講話的部分（有前後引號的句子）都是用現在式，而旁白或敘述事情都是用過去式，這就是過去式的用途，幫助我們清楚了解事件發生的時候。

月份的英文

　　真是生於憂患死於安樂！可憐的蟋蟀兄帕拉尼，凍死在冰冷的十二月（December）。現在的氣候多變，有時候說翻臉就翻臉，還真的必須未雨綢繆，才能因應無情的大自然力量啊！那麼，大家既然學了 December，其他月份的英文當然也不能不知道吧！英文的十二月份分別是：

一月 JANUARY　　FEBRUARY 二月

三月 MARCH　　APRIL 四月

五月 MAY I LOVE YOU MOM.　　JUNE 六月

七月 July　　August 八月

九月 SePEMBER　　OCTOBER 十月

十一月 November　　December 十二月

親子英文共讀筆記欄

可以把不熟悉的
單字片語寫在這邊喔!

Unit 13
巴蛇吞象

精選句型 It happened that + S + V...

I don't think so.

no wonder + 子句

片語解析 catch a cold

文法解析 過去進行式

我的天啊 !!

Unit 13

Pakistan Snake Swallows Elephant

"Are you all right, Buzz?"

也可以用 O.K. 取代，表示「一切都好」

"I feel sick as a dog; maybe I should see a doctor."

這邊用「像一隻狗」來形容前面的sick（生病的），表示「生重病」

After Buzz came back from a picnic yesterday, he

kept moaning and crying in his room, and he was

keep + Ving 表示「持續某一個動作」

unwilling to go out of his room or tell his mother what

它的反義就是willing（願意的）

happened. His mom thought he caught a cold and it

happened that her mother's friend Dr. Conrad, was

boarding in their house. So, he walked toward the

它還可表示「登機」喔

room door, knocked on it and asked if the kid needed

some advice.

Pause & Answer 動動腦

1. What was wrong with Buzz?

（Buzz 怎麼了？）

解答在 P.227

184

巴蛇吞象

「巴蛇，你還好吧？」

「我覺得我生重病了；或許我該去看醫生了……」

自從巴蛇昨天野餐回來後，他就在他房裡一直一把鼻涕一把眼淚地呻吟著，且他不願意走出房間，或告訴媽媽發生了什麼事。媽媽以為巴蛇感冒了，而正好媽媽的醫生朋友康拉德寄住在他家，所以他走到巴蛇的房間門口，敲敲門，然後詢問這孩子是否需要些建議。

Keywords 關鍵字詞

1	snake	[snek]	n.	蛇
2	swallow	[`swɑlo]	v.	吞
3	elephant	[`ɛləfənt]	n.	象
4	picnic	[`pɪknɪk]	n.	野餐
5	moan	[mon]	v.	哀嚎
6	unwilling	[ʌn`wɪlɪŋ]	adj.	不願意的
7	board	[bord]	v.	寄宿
8	knock	[nɑk]	v.	敲
9	advice	[əd`vaɪs]	n.	忠告，建議

picnic

moan

advice

充 電 站

生病或感冒的時候，只會說 I'm sick. 或 I have a cold. 嗎？要是你喉嚨痛、頭暈、想吐或是拉肚子（前面「鈴鐺貓」那個單元學過喔！）又該怎麼表達呢？我們一次把它學起來吧！喉嚨痛，可以說 I got a sore throat.，頭暈，可以說 I'm feeling dizzy.，想吐的話，是 I'm feeling like vomiting. 那麼，流鼻涕，我們可以說 runny nose。

"Are you O.K., kid?" Conrad asked. "Well, I don't think so." Buzz answered.

"So, can you tell me how you feel right now?" Conrad

當我們要開始與人交談時，可以用So這個字來打開話匣子

asked.

"I feel dizzy, weak and cold," Buzz said.

"Um, do you have a runny nose or the runs?" Conrad

「流鼻水」也可以說running nose

asked.

"No, not at all." Buzz shook his head.

這是shake的過去式，後面受詞如果是hand，就變成
「握手」的意思囉

"So, let me check your blood pressure. Take a deep

「量血壓」的「量」可以用check 這個動詞喔

breath, please?" Conrad said, and he proceeded to

do a physical examination.

它的反義字就是mental（心理的）

Pause & Answer 動動腦

2. What did the doctor do for Buzz?
（這位醫生為巴蛇做什麼？）

解答在 P.227

康拉德問：「你還好吧，小朋友？」

巴蛇回答：「嗯，我想我不是很好。」

康拉德又問：「那你能告訴我你現在覺得如何嗎？」

巴蛇回答：「我覺得頭暈目眩、虛弱而且很冷。」

康拉德問：「那你會流鼻水或者是拉肚子嗎？」

巴蛇搖頭說：「沒有，都沒有。」

康拉德說：「嗯，那讓我來檢查你的血壓。來，請深呼吸。」然後他繼續做身體檢查。

Keywords 關鍵字詞

10	dizzy	[`dɪzɪ]	adj.	暈眩的
11	runny nose	[`rʌnɪ] [noz]	n.	流鼻水
12	have the runs		ph.	拉肚子
13	blood pressure	[blʌd] [`prɛʃɚ]	n.	血壓
14	deep breath	[dip] [brɛθ]	n.	深呼吸
15	proceed	[prə`sid]	v.	繼續進行
16	physical	[`fɪzɪkl̩]	adj.	身體的
17	examination	[ɪg͵zæmə`neʃən]	n.	檢查

dizzy

runny nose

deep breath

原來 check 這個動詞，除了當「檢查」之外，也可以拿來「量」血壓呢！此外，看醫生之前，通常要先量體溫，看看有沒有發燒，這時，護士可能會對你說：Let me take your temperature.（讓我替你量體溫）。所以，這邊的 check 也可以用 take 取代喔！另外，中醫師替病人把脈來診斷，英文就可以說：feel your pulse（替你把脈）。

"That's strange. Everything's OK. But I guess you might eat something bad, right?"

"Well, ah..., I did eat some... maybe a bit big things.

did是do的過去式，但是在這裡表示「的確」的意思

Maybe you can come in to get the picture." Buzz said.

這不是「得到一張照片／圖」的意思，而是「明白」意思

Then, the whole neighborhood could hear the doctor's sharp scream.

"My goodness, no wonder you feel bad. Honestly, tell

最近流行話「我的老天鵝啊！」就可以用它來表示

me what you ate."

"I... I ate a rabbit, two frogs, a dozen of eggs, a

小朋友們應該知道這個動物是十二生肖之一吧！那麼這個句子中還以有哪些動物也是呢？

horse, a boy, a monkey and an elephant."

Pause & Answer 動動腦

3. What did Buss eat yesterday?
（巴蛇昨天吃了什麼？）

解答在 P.227

「那就怪了。一切都沒問題啊！但我猜想你可能吃了些不乾淨的東西，是吧？」

巴蛇說：「嗯…哦…我的確是吃了一些 ... 也許有點大的東西…嗯，也許你進來看看就會知道了。」

然後，整個街坊鄰居都能夠聽到這醫生尖銳的叫聲。

「我的天啊！難怪你會覺得不舒服，告訴我你到底吃了什麼！」

「我…我吃了一隻兔子、兩隻青蛙、一打雞蛋、一四馬、一個小男孩、一隻猴子和一頭大象。」

Keywords 關鍵字詞

18	a bit	[ə`bɪt]	adv. 一點，些微
19	get the picture		ph. 探個究竟，了解
20	neighborhood	[`nebɚ͵hʊd]	n. 街坊鄰居
21	sharp	[ʃɑrp]	adj. 尖銳的
22	wonder	[`wʌndɚ]	n. 驚奇
23	honestly	[`ɑnɪstlɪ]	adv. 誠實地，老實說
24	frog	[frɑg]	n. 青蛙
25	monkey	[`mʌŋkɪ]	n. 猴子

sharp

wonder

充電站

neighbor 這個字本來是「鄰居」的意思，是可數名詞（後面可加 -s），而 neighborhood 在這邊則是指「鄰近地區的人們」，所以這兩個字就有點像 person 和 people 的關係。不過，當 neighborhood 作「鄰近地區」時，是可以數的，比如說，The blackout took place in all the neighborhoods nearby.（這附近所有鄰近地區都停電了。）

189

Useful Expressions 精選句型

It happened that + S + V… 碰巧…

→ It happened that they saw the accident on their way home.

碰巧他們在回家的路上看到這起意外。

I don't think so. 我不這麼認為。

→ A: Can you do this? B: Yes, I think so.

反過來說，I think so. 可用來表示「同意」。

A：你可以做這件事嗎？ B：是的，我是這麼認為的。

no wonder + 子句 難怪…

→ She has a good husband. It's no wonder that she looks so happy.

也可以用 No wonder 取代

她有個好丈夫。難怪她看起來這麼幸福。

● "It happened that..." 這個句型中的 It 是個「虛主詞」，代替後面 that 子句 (真主詞)。就好像 "It is true that..." (... 是真的。) 這樣的句型。

● so (所以) 是個副詞，用來修飾動詞 think。不過在意義上，so 這個字是代表前面說過的事情。比如這裡的 I think so. 就等於 "I think I can do this."

● wonder 可以當名詞，表示「驚奇 (的人事物)」，當動詞時，就表示「對 ... 感到驚奇」或「很想知道 ...」。所以 no wonder (沒有驚奇) 就是「難怪 ...」的意思了。最後，我們來練習看看下面這句話的英文怎麼說吧：
「難怪這麼多人想到室內游泳池去。外面天氣真的太熱了！」

解答在 P.227

catch a cold

- 什麼叫「捕捉一個寒冷」？

cold 通常當形容詞表示「寒冷的」沒錯，但它也可以當名詞，表示「感冒」。想想看，晚上吹冷氣睡覺踢被子，就很有機會catch a cold（感冒）。另外 catch 也可以替換成 have 喔！接下來，我們就再來看看還有什麼跟 cold 有關的片語吧！

Last Christmas was so chilly that many of my friends caught a cold.
去年聖誕節時冷到讓我很多朋友都感冒了。

The haunted house made me get cold feet.

中文所說的因為害怕而「軟腳」，英文可不能說成soft feet 喔！

這鬼屋讓我兩腳發軟。

I tried to please him, but he just gave me the cold shoulder.

中文裡的「熱臉貼冷屁股」，用 cold shoulder 就對啦！
我試著要取悅他，但他卻冷漠回應我。

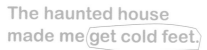

過去進行式

這篇故事是改編自中國古代的《山海經》。俗話説得好,「人心不足蛇吞象。」就是比喻太貪心的人,就好像一條蛇想要把大象吞到肚子裡一樣,不自量力。就像咱們的巴蛇,這次也未免太貪心了吧!竟然吞了這麼多東西,難怪會肚子不舒服,而又是哀嚎又是痛哭了老半天:…he was moaning and crying…。

看到這邊這句話,大家會不會有一個疑問?我們為什麼不用過去簡單式就好了,也就是 "…he moaned and cried…"。另外,剛剛那句話看起來很像現在進行式,不過又好像不太一樣,那是什麼句了呢?

雖然説事情都有先後順序,不過這次老師想要先回答第二個問題:這是什麼句子?其實只要稍微想一想就可以猜出它的名稱,不信的話我們就來試試看,老師先拿長得跟它很像的現在進行式來給大家看:

He is moaning and crying.
接下來比較一下文章裡的句子
…he was moaning and crying…

在老師的得力助手紅文字軍團的幫助之下,大家有發現了什麼東西嗎?沒錯,其實兩句只有一個地方不同,也就是 be 動詞的地方:一個是現在式,一個是過去式。既然只差一個地方,那麼是否可以推敲出名稱來了?答對了,這就叫「過去進行式」。過去進行式的用法和現在進行式完全一樣,唯一需要注意的地方就只有 be 動詞,記得要使用過去式(am/ is → was,are → were)。

接下來回答第一個問題，為什麼不用「過去簡單式」就好了，而要用過去進行式？其實原本「進行式」所要強調的就是一個「動作的持續性」，而過去簡單式則只是描述「過去曾經發生過」的事情。在故事裡我們就是要強調他「一直哀嚎、一直哭鬧」，大家閱讀的時候才會真的感覺到巴蛇的問題很嚴重，要是只用簡單的一句 he moaned and cried，那種可憐的 fu 就完全表現不出來吧！

所以，「現在進行式」是指「一個動作在現在的時間點正在進行」，那「過去進行式」當然就是指「一個動作在過去的某一個時間點正在進行」。

現在，我們就來驗收一下。下面有五個句子，哪些句子要用「過去進行式」來表示呢？

1. 王先生正在田裡種菜。
2. 她正在公園裡散步。
3. 昨晚八點時，他們正在拜訪一位老朋友。
4. 我今天早上已經看了這場棒球賽。
5. 爸爸回來的時候，媽媽正在煮飯。

答案揭曉囉！第 3 和第 5 句。它們的英文是：

At eight o'clock last night, they were visiting an old friend.
When Daddy was back, mom was cooking.

從以上幾個句子，我們可以歸納出兩個簡單的結論，那就是，「過去進行式」用在兩種情境中：

1. 過去的某個時間點，某動作正在進行。→ 第 3 句
2. 在過去的時間裡，當某一個動作發生時，另一動作正在進行。
   → 第 5 句

字詞一籮筐

各種「感冒症狀」的英文

感冒的症狀不外就是頭痛、發燒、痠痛、鼻塞、咳嗽、打噴嚏、腹瀉、胃脹氣、喉嚨痛。大家一起來找出那一張圖搭配哪一種症狀吧！

(1) headache 頭疼	(2) have a fever 發燒	(3) ache in the shoulder 肩膀痠痛
(4) stuffy nose 鼻塞	(5) cough 咳嗽	(6) sneeze 打噴嚏
(7) diarrhea 腹瀉	(8) stomach gas 胃脹氣	(9) sore throat 喉嚨痛

親子英文共讀筆記欄

可以把不熟悉的
單字片語寫在這邊喔！

Unit 14
醜小鴨

精選句型 A + be + adj-er than + B

Looks like + 子句

It is + adj + of + 人

片語解析 take a shower

文法解析 對等連接詞

Stop! Looks like you're equal!

The Ugly Duckling

The Ugly Duckling always thinks she

is one of the ugliest animals in the whole
　　　　　　ugly 的形容詞最高級。去 -y 後加字尾 -iest

world. So, she goes to take baths at Beitou Beauty
　　　　　　「洗澡」（take a bath）或「沖澡」（take a shower）的動詞都用 take

Hot Springs every day. She wants to become prettier
　　　　　　pretty 的形容詞比較級，去 -y 後加字尾 -ier（下個單元就會介紹喔！）

than a swan. One day, she met one at the pool. "Hey

you! Take care not to slip on the wet ground. Wait...
　　　　要別人「小心注意」或「保重」可以說 Take care!

you are a swan, aren't you? You look so charming! I

think you must have many admirers." Ugly Duckling
　　　　　　　　　　　　動詞 admire 表示「仰慕」的意思

asked excitedly.

 Pause & Answer 動動腦

1. Why does Ugly Duckling go to Beitou Beauty Hot
   Springs every day?
   （醜小鴨為什麼要每天去北投美人溫泉？）

解答在 P.227

醜小鴨

　　醜小鴨總認為她是世界上最醜的動物之一，所以她每天都去「北投美人溫泉」泡湯，她想要變得比天鵝還美麗，有一天，她在水池邊遇到了一隻天鵝。

　　醜小鴨興奮地問：「欸你！小心地上很濕，別滑倒了。等等，妳是一隻天鵝，對不對？妳看起來好迷人喔！我想妳一定有許多愛慕者吧！」。

Keywords 關鍵字詞

1	ugly	[`ʌglɪ]	adj. 醜的
2	animal	[`ænəml̩]	n. 動物
3	pretty	[`prɪtɪ]	adj. 漂亮的
4	beauty	[`bjutɪ]	n. 美人
5	slip	[slɪp]	v. 滑倒，滑行
6	wet	[wɛt]	adj. 濕的
7	charming	[`tʃɑrmɪŋ]	adj. 迷人的
8	admirer	[əd`maɪrɚ]	n. 仰慕者
9	excited	[ɪk`saɪtɪd]	adj. 感到興奮的

ugly

beauty

slip

beauty（美；美人），形容詞是 beautiful（美麗的），如果要說，「這個人很沒有美感」，英文就是 The man has no feeling for beauty.。英文裡有很多大家耳熟能詳的俗諺，都用到 beauty 這個字喔！比方說 Beauty is only skin deep.（美貌是膚淺的）；Beauty is in the eye of the beholder.（情人眼裡出西施。）；Beauty fades like a flower.（紅顏薄命。）

"Thanks. My name is Linda, and you are...? " the

英文口語中常常用肯定句型來代替「疑問句」

swan replied. "I'm Ugly Duckling. Nice to meet you."

跟前面學過的 What's up! 一樣，都是「打招呼」用語

Ugly Duckling said as she soaked one of her feet in

the water. "Me, too. I'd like to take a shower first."

Linda answered politely. "Oops! Looks like there isn't

any hot water." Linda said. "Well then, just come here

and I'll help you scrub your back," Ugly Duckling

這是運用了「help + 人 + 原形V」（幫助某人做…）的句型

said. "Okay," Linda answered.

Then Ugly Duckling asked Linda about many things

補充句型：「ask + 人 + about + 事情」（問某人某件事）

like beauty salons, spas and cosmetics.

Pause & Answer 動動腦

2. What happened when Swan Linda was ready to take
   a shower?

   （當天鵝琳達要去沖澡時，發生了什麼事？）

解答在 P.227

天鵝回答：「謝謝，我叫作琳達，妳是…？」醜小鴨一邊將一隻腳浸泡在水中，一邊說：「我叫醜小鴨，很高興認識妳。」琳達很有禮貌地回答：「我也很高興認識妳。我想先沖個澡。」「糟糕！好像沒有熱水了！」醜小鴨：「那妳過來這邊吧！我幫妳刷背！」琳達說：「好啊！」

接著醜小鴨問了琳達許多事情，像是美容院、水療和化妝品等。

Keywords 關鍵字詞

10	swan	[swɑn]	n.	天鵝
11	soak	[sok]	v.	浸泡
12	feet	[fit]	n.	腳（foot 的複數）
13	scrub	[skrʌb]	v.	擦洗
14	back	[bæk]	n.	背部
15	salon	[sə`lɑn]	n.	沙龍，（營業性的）廳、院
16	spa	[spɑ]	n.	水療，礦泉，浴場
17	cosmetics	[kɑz`mɛtɪks]	n.	化妝品

soak

cosmetics

scrub

充電站

英文裡最正式的問候語非 "How do you do?" 莫屬了，不過現在比較少用，因為它太過正式、呆板。現在，初次見面的彼此，比較常用的說法是 "Nice to meet you."。若是很熟的朋友，那非正式的問候通常就是簡單的 "Hi!"，而回應的話也說 "Hi!" 即可，接著可以再問對方 "How are you lately?"、"How's going?" 等，都是「最近好嗎？」的意思。

"It's so kind of you. Do you come here every day?"

Linda said. "Yes, because I want to be as attractive

as you! Is there any secret to this?" Duckling replied.

「…的秘訣」要用介系詞to，不是用of喔！

"Don't be silly. You're still young. You will grow up and

become pretty as me." Linda patted Ugly Duckling on

也可以說 as pretty as（和…一樣漂亮）

the shoulder proudly. Then Duckling said, "By the

way, I have coupons to an aerobics class. Maybe we

coupon 也是 ticket（票）的一種，所以搭配 to 使用

can go together someday." "Sounds great! But is the

常用來表示「贊同」或「樂意接受」的意思

class hard? Actually I don't like to study…" the swan

questioned.

Pause & Answer 動動腦

3. What did Linda think about Duckling's invitation to
   the aerobics class?
   （琳達對於小鴨的有氧舞蹈課邀約有什麼看法？）

解答在 P.227

琳達說：「妳人真好啊！妳每天都會來這裡嗎？」

醜小鴨回答：「是啊！因為我想要變得跟妳一樣有魅力。這有什麼訣竅嗎？」

琳達驕傲地拍拍醜小鴨的肩膀說：「別傻了！妳還很年輕，妳會長大，而且會和我一樣漂亮的。」

這時小鴨說：「對了，我這邊有幾張有氧舞蹈課的優待券，或許我們哪天可以一起去喔！」

「聽起來很棒！不過那個課會很難嗎？我其實沒有很喜歡念書耶…」天鵝問道。

Keywords 關鍵字詞

18	attractive	[ə`træktɪv]	adj.	吸引人的
19	secret	[`sikrɪt]	n.	祕訣
20	silly	[`sɪlɪ]	adj.	傻的，愚蠢的
21	pat	[pæt]	v.	輕拍
22	shoulder	[`ʃoldɚ]	n.	肩膀
23	proud	[praʊd]	adj.	驕傲的
24	coupon	[`kupɑn]	n.	優待券
25	aerobics	[ˏeə`robɪks]	n.	有氧舞蹈
26	question	[`kwɛstʃən]	v.	詢問

充電站

其實「傻」和「笨」本來就有「程度」上的差別，英文裡的 silly，就是我們中文所講的「傻傻的」，通常強調的是「不認真」（not serious）或「欠缺考量」（not think carefully），而 stupid（笨的）這個字比較帶有「令人瞧不起的愚蠢」、「令人想責罵的愚蠢」的負面意義。

Useful Expressions 精選句型

A + be + 比較級的adj + than + B

A 比 B 還要更⋯

→ Mom was more shocked than Dad when they saw

這是過去分詞當形容詞用，表示「震驚的」

their house was all a mess.

當他們看見房子一團亂時，媽媽比爸爸還要震驚。

Looks like + 完整句子 看來⋯

→ Looks like our worries are unnecessary.

還記得 Unit 9 的 necessity（必需品）嗎？unnecessary 就是
「沒必要的」。

He's studying hard now.

看來我們的憂慮是沒必要的。他正在用功呢！

It is + adj + of + 人 (+ to-V) 某人⋯

→ It's so kind of you to help me.

你人真好，還幫我忙。

Sentence Patterns 句型解析

● 這是「比較級」的句型,我們將在下一課的文法單元進行詳細解説。在這邊大家只要先記得「形容詞比較級 + than」這個句型。而這個「形容詞比較級」又分成「adj. + -er」和「more + adj.」兩種喔!

● 以 Looks like (或 Sounds like) 為開頭的句子,通常用於口語中,前面省略了「虛主詞」it,可還原成 It looks / sounds like + 完整句子。

● 首先,我們要知道一個基本句型: be + adj + of/for + 人。形容「人」的時候就用 of ,形容「事物」的時候就用 to。比如説:It's lazy of you not to help. (你都不幫忙,真是懶惰。)、It's still possible for you to win the game. (你還是有可能贏得比賽。)

最後,我們來看看下面這句的英文怎麼説吧:

「雙方勢均力敵。看來他們要分出勝負有點困難。」

"Both are of equal strength.

_____

_____

解答在 P.227

take a shower

- 什麼叫「拿走一陣雨」？

shower 本來是「陣雨」的意思。我們可以想像,從「蓮蓬頭」(shower head)降下來的水,是不是很像「陣雨」?所以 take a shower 不是說下雨的時候跑去外面去淋雨,而是「淋浴」的意思,而 take a bath 一般就是指「洗澡」,因為 bath 本身就有「浴缸」的意思。

He's taking a shower now.
他現在正在淋浴。

How long do you need to take a bath?
你洗澡需要花多少時間呢?

She likes to enjoy a relaxing afternoon in a bath.
表示「泡澡中」
她喜歡在泡澡中享受午後的休閒時光。

對等連接詞

　　每天幻想要變成天鵝的醜小鴨，每天都去「美人溫泉」泡湯，只希望自己能夠變得跟心目中的偶像一樣漂亮，結果竟然真的遇到了天鵝琳達，而且還傳授她許多美容的心得，像是美容院、水療和化妝品（beauty salon, spa and cosmetic）的事情，想必醜小鴨將來一定會變成一隻大美鴨！不過這隻天鵝竟然以為有氧舞蹈課是需要讀書的課，可見,美貌真的是膚淺的啊！

　　當然這個故事的重點，不是要教我們如何在泡湯的時候打聽愛美情報，既然老師這邊又把紅字秀出來，那就一定有特別的用意囉！沒錯，這邊就要介紹一個新朋友給大家認識：對等連接詞。

　　對等連接詞聽起來真的很抽象，不如我們換個角度來看好了，我們可以把它想像成是英文裡面的某種膠水，可以把句子或者是單字黏在一起，不過對等連接詞有一個特別的地方在於它只能黏相同性質的東西，所以一邊黏單字，另外一邊就要黏單字；一邊黏句子，另外一邊也要黏句子，總之一定要有「對等」的關係。基本上，對等連接詞就只有下面這 5 個：

對等連接詞				
and	but	or	nor	yet
和，以及	但是	或者	也不	但；卻

接下來我們用幾個例子來看看對等連接詞的功能吧！

	單字黏單字	句子黏句子
and	I have soap and a towel.	I like to go to Beauty Hot Spring and he likes to go to Healthy Hot Spring.
	我有肥皂和浴巾。	我喜歡去美人溫泉，而他喜歡去健康溫泉。
but	This hot spring is good but expensive.	This hot spring is hot but it feels good.
	這個溫泉很好但是也很貴。	這個溫泉很燙可是很舒服。
or	You can go to the hot spring or cold spring.	You can take it by yourself or I will take it for you.
	你可以去泡溫泉或冷泉。	你可以自己來拿或者是我幫你拿。
nor	I didn't talk nor write to her.	You don't like him, nor do I.
	我沒有和她說話，也沒有寫信給她。	你不喜歡他，我也是。
yet	The weather was cold, yet sunny.	Your dress looks strange, yet I likes it.
	天氣很冷，不過很晴朗。	妳的洋裝看起來很怪，但我喜歡。

★ 注意：要先熟悉 and、but 和 or 這三個最基本的對等連接詞。而 yet 相當於 but，但差別在於 yet 可以當副詞用，而 nor 必須在否定句裡使用。

在美容院中

　　除了泡美人湯，做做 spa，跳跳有氧舞蹈，小鴨和琳達天鵝還聊到一個地方是可以讓自己變漂亮的。沒錯，那就是 beauty salon（美容院）。下面這張圖就是美容院內常見的人或物，大家一起來找出它們的英文吧！

(1)	steamer 蒸氣機
(2)	recliner 躺椅
(3)	scissors 剪刀
(4)	clipper 推剪機
(5)	blow dryer 吹風機
(6)	mirror 鏡子
(7)	customer 客人
(8)	comb 梳子
(9)	hairdresser 美髮師

親子英文共讀筆記欄

可以把不熟悉的
單字片語寫在這邊喔！

Unit 15
龜兔賽跑

He's really ready to argue!

The Turtle and The Rabbit

fix本來是「修理」的意思，所以不管是「梳頭髮、「綁頭髮」…等都可以用 fix fair 表示喔！

The Rabbit was fixing his hair before his

last match with the Turtle began. The

score was tied at 1:1. This third game

字面意思是「綁在1比1」，就是「不分勝負」

was to decide who is faster, and it was held at

Disneyland. The rule is this: whoever first takes all

意思是「無論誰」，可等於 no matter who

the rides and crosses the finish line will be the

winner. As usual, the Rabbit was far ahead of the

game, again. So, he decided to enjoy the fancy hotel -

the Turtle ordered a room before the game.

也可用 book 取代。除了「預訂」的意思之外，到餐廳「點菜」時，也可以說 I'd like to order…

 Pause & Answer 動動腦

1. Where was Rabbit and Turtle's third race held?
   （兔子和烏龜的第三場賽跑在哪裡舉行？）

解答在 P.227

龜兔賽跑

　　在兔子和烏龜的最後一場比賽開始前，兔子正在整理他的頭髮。目前比數是一比一。這第三場比賽將決定誰比較快，且它是在迪士尼樂園舉辦。規則是這樣：誰先玩遍所有設施，然後跨過終點線就是贏家。一如往常地，兔子又遙遙領先了，所以他決定先享受一下那精緻的旅館 — 烏龜在賽前就訂好一間房了。

Keywords 關鍵字詞

1	fix one's hair		ph. 弄頭髮
2	match	[mætʃ]	n. （兩方的）比賽、對抗賽
3	score	[skor]	n. 分數
4	tie	[taɪ]	v. 打結，打成平手
5	rule	[rul]	n. 規則
6	finish line	[`fɪnɪʃ] [laɪn]	n. 終點線
7	winner	[`wɪnɚ]	n. 贏家
8	as usual	[æz`juʒʊəl]	adv. 一如往常
9	order	[`ɔrdɚ]	v. 預訂

充電站

原來「弄」頭髮的動詞可以用 fix 來表示呢！不過去理髮時，總不能只會說 "I want to fix my hair." 吧！如果要告訴美髮師說，「我要洗和剪」，就可以說 I'd like to get a wash and a cut.。其它像燙髮 (get a perm)、修短一點 (have a trim)、染髮 (a dye)，甚至「挑染」(highlights)、護髮 (a hair care session) 也都相當實用喔！

"Hah hah..., let me take a nap. The slow Turtle will

也可以替換成 It will take the slow Turtle…

spend at least three days reaching here," Rabbit

talked to himself heartily, when the phone was

ringing... "This is Rabbit speaking. Who's this?"

當醫院病患有事「按鈴」呼叫醫生或護士前來，也可以用這個動詞喔！

Rabbit said. "I'm Turtle. You're ready to sleep again?"

Turtle asked.

"Sure, I'm in pajamas, drinking a cocktail and lying on

lie這個動詞的進行式很特別，不可寫成 lieing 喔！

a nice bed. But don't worry. Even if I sleep in, I have

enough time waiting for you," the rabbit answered

這句話學起來：I'll wait for you.（我會等你。）

lazily and hung up the phone.

Pause & Answer 動動腦

2. What did Rabbit wear when he answered the phone
   made by Turtle?

   （當兔子接到烏龜打來的電話時，他穿著什麼？）

解答在 P.227

「哈……讓我小睡片刻吧。那隻小慢龜至少要花個三天才會抵達這裡。」兔子開心地自言自語著，這時電話響了。兔子說：「你好，我是兔子，請問哪位？」「我是烏龜啦！你又準備要去睡覺了嗎？」烏龜問。

「當然，我現在穿著睡衣、喝著雞尾酒，躺在一張舒服的床上。不過別擔心，即使我睡到自然醒，我還有很多時間來等你啦！」兔子懶洋洋地回答後，就掛斷電話了。

Keywords 關鍵字詞

10	nap	[næp]	n.	小睡
11	at least	[æt`list]	adv.	至少
12	reach	[ritʃ]	v.	到達
13	pajamas	[pə`dʒæməs]	n.	連身睡衣
14	cocktail	[`kɑk‚tel]	n.	雞尾酒
15	lie	[laɪ]	v.	躺
16	sleep in	[`slip‚ɪn]	v.	睡到自然醒
17	hang up	[`hæŋ‚ʌp]	v.	掛斷電話

nap

pajamas

hang up

充 電 站

lie這個動詞，有「躺」也有「說謊」的意思，但比較麻煩的是，這兩種意思的時態變化不一樣。lie（躺）→lay→lain→lying；lie（說謊）→lied→lied→lying。還沒完，lay這個動詞也有「放置」（=put）的意思，它的動詞變化是：lay→laid→laying。這樣大家對於 lie 和 lay 的動詞變化了解了嗎？別再傻傻分不清囉！

215

Of course, victory will finally belong to Turtle. But

how? It's impossible for Rabbit to fall asleep for 3

還記得上個單元學過的 for 用來形容「事情」，而形容「人」的話，要用 of 喔！

days! In fact, Turtle thought more than Rabbit. He

「想比較多」的意思，如果是「想太多」就可以說 think too much。

knew Rabbit would regard the match as an easy win.

as 這個介系詞與前面的 regard 有連動關係喔！

So he booked a room for Rabbit and put sleeping pills

in his cocktail... "Why are you in such a bad mood?

Did you get up on the wrong side of the bed?"

相反地，如果起床時心情很好，可以說 get up on the "right" side of the bed

"That's strange! How could I sleep for almost four

days? That's crazy!"

Pause & Answer 動動腦

3. Why did rabbit oversleep again?

（兔子為什麼又睡過頭了？）

解答在 P.227

當然，勝利最後是屬於烏龜的。但怎麼贏的？兔子根本不可能睡三天吧！事實上，烏龜想得比兔子更遠！他早就知道兔子會認為他可以輕鬆獲勝，所以他才幫兔子訂了房間，並且在雞尾酒中放了安眠藥⋯「你幹嘛心情這麼不好？你是吃錯藥嗎？」

「怪了！我怎麼會睡了快四天啊！真是太扯了！」

Keywords 關鍵字詞

18	victory	[ˋvɪktərɪ]	n.	勝利
19	belong to	[bəˋlɔŋ] [tu]	v.	屬於
20	impossible	[ɪmˋpɑsəbl]	adj.	不可能的
21	in fact	[ɪnˋfækt]	adv.	事實上
22	regard	[rɪˋgɑrd]	v.	把⋯看作，認為
23	sleeping pill	[ˋslipɪŋ] [pɪl]	n.	安眠藥
24	mood	[mud]	n.	心情
25	get up on the wrong side of the bed		ph.	莫名心情鬱悶，起床氣

victory

get up on the wrong side of the bed

充電站

大家聽過「起床氣」嗎？簡單說就是「一早起床時就奇蒙子不爽」（可能是做了個令人生氣的夢吧！），這對於旁邊的人來說，就會覺得這人怎麼莫名其妙不高興。所以 get up on the wrong side of the bed 這個片語也可引申為「心情鬱悶」（in a bad mood）。相反地，如果要表示「心情好」，只要把這邊的 wrong 改成 right 就行囉！

217

Useful Expressions 精選句型

S + be + to-V   目的是…；將會…

→ You are to decide which way to go.
  你該決定要走哪一條路了。

S + be ready + for N / to-V   準備要…

→ He's so angry! Looks like there'll be a fight there.
  他好生氣呢！看來那裡有人要吵架了。

He's really ready to argue!

S (人) + be in a good / bad mood   某人心情好／壞

→ Peter was in a bad mood because he failed the test.
  彼得因為考試考壞而心情不好。

誰叫你不用功！

Sentence Patterns 句型解析

● 在英文裡，be 動詞 + 不定詞 (to-V) 主要有三種意義：1. 表示「目的」或「意圖」；2. 表示「將來」（相當於未來式助動詞 will）；3. 表示「義務」或「必須」（相當於助動詞 must）。

● be ready 就是「準備好了」。在比賽開始前，我們常會聽到裁判說 Are you ready? Go! (你準備好了嗎？開始！) 它的後面還可以再加上「for + N」或「to + V」表示「為 ... 做好準備」。

● 首先「處於…心情」的介系詞要用 in。另外，mood 的後面其實還可以在加「to + V」來表示「有／沒心情做某事」。比如說：He's in no mood to eat. (他現在沒心情吃東西。)

最後，我們來看看下面這句話的英文怎麼說吧：

她帶我來這裡的目的就是要買鑽戒。

Her purpose of bringing me here _____.

解答在 P.227

He's not ready to decide!

ahead of the game

● 什麼叫「在比賽的前頭」？

head 是「頭」，所以 ahead（在前面）應該很好理解吧！那麼 ahead of the game 其實就是「在比賽中領先」的意思，更抽象意義而言，它也有「處於有利位置」的意思喔！

We need to stay ahead of the game for long-time (survival).

[səˋvaɪvl]，表示「生存」，動詞是 survive

我們必須保持在有利的位置，才能夠長時間生存。

- -

Andy is now far ahead of the game while Peter is still trying to (catch up).

表示「趕上」

安迪現在遙遙領先，而彼得仍試圖趕上。

- -

He called his father (ahead of time), and

表示「提早」，相當於 in advance 或 beforehand

said "Happy Father's Day!" to him.

他提早打電話給他爸爸，跟他說聲：「父親節快樂！」。

220

比較級

首先，恭喜烏龜最後還是智取兔子，獲得了勝利，誰跑得比較快已經不重要了，不過誰比較足智多謀，或是說比較深謀遠慮，大家心中自有評斷了吧！說到「比較」、「比來比去」，「比較」敏感的讀者應該能感覺到，老師又再鋪什麼梗了？哈哈，被發現了！這次不需要動用紅色字軍團也可以猜到老師想要講的是什麼，那就是比較級啦！

大家從小到大都喜歡比較，比較高矮、胖瘦、美醜、考試成績，或是誰跑得比較快，所以我們現在就來看要怎樣用英文表示才會感覺「比較」厲害。

其實比較級算是形容詞三種「級」的其中之一，主要是用來比較兩個人或者是兩個東西，表達其中一個比另外一個「更……」，通常會跟 than 一起使用，套用在以下這個句型：

某人或某事物 + 動詞 + 比較級 + than + 某人或某事物

The rabbit can run **faster** than the turtle.

The turtle is **smarter** than the rabbit.

不過比較級真正棘手的地方還沒出現，
我們繼續往下看吧！

當我們使用比較級的時候，形容詞本身是需要變化的。基本上，單音節的字在字尾加上 er，雙音節以上的字則視情況加上 more 或 er。聽起來好像很複雜，不過別擔心，老師已經把這些變化整理成表格給大家參考。

音節數	行容詞類型	如何變化	範例
單音節	單母音 + 單子音	重覆字尾子音再加 r	big 大 → bigger 更大
	字尾為 e	直接加 r	close 近 → closer 更近
	其他	直接加 er	fast 快 → faster 更快
雙音節	字尾為y	去 y 加 ier	easy 簡單→ easier 更簡單
	字尾非 y	字前面加上 more	famous 有名→ more famous 更有名
三音節			beautiful 漂亮→ more beautiful 更漂亮

最後，還有一些不團結的份子！像過去式一樣，有些形容詞的比較級變化也是不規則的，以下提供幾種常見的不規則變化：

bad	→	worse	good	→	better
well	→	better	far（距離）	→	farther
far（程度）	→	further	little	→	less
many	→	more	much	→	more

在遊樂園中

小朋友們常去兒童樂園或是其他遊樂園（amusement park）玩嗎？大家都知道那些遊樂設施的英文怎麼說嗎？

(1)	Merry Go Round 旋轉木馬
(2)	Bumper Cars 碰碰車
(3)	Ferris Wheel 摩天輪
(4)	Roller Coaster 雲霄飛車
(5)	Drop Ride 自由落體
(6)	Spinning Tea Cups 旋轉茶杯
(7)	Haunted House 鬼屋
(8)	Pirate Ship 海盜船

(9)	Go-Kart 卡丁車	10	Evolution 風火輪

解答篇 Answer Keys

Unit 1

p.16   **1. For three hours.**（達 3 小時之久）

p.18   **2. He answered slowly and lazily.**（他緩慢且覽散地回答。）

p.20   **3. He brushed his teeth, washed his face, and studied his schoolwork.**（他刷牙、洗臉，然後做功課。）

p.23   **4. It's time to go to bed. You'd better sleep and get up early, or you will be late tomorrow again.**

Unit 2

p.30   **1. Because the belled cat is coming soon.**（因為鈴鐺貓要來了。）

p.32   **2. For ten minutes.**（十分鐘之久）

p.34   **3. Tissue paper.**（衛生紙）

Unit 3

p.44   **1. Once a week.**（一週一次）

p.46   **2. To buy his mother a birthday gift.**（為了幫媽媽買生日禮物）

p.48   **3. NT$1,200.**（新台幣 1,200 元）

Unit 4

p.58   **1. Next to the pine tree.**（在松樹旁）

p.60   **2. He was looking for his cane.**（他在找尋他的拐杖。）

p.62   **3. If his horse were not missing, he would not go out to look for it, and then he would stay in his house that came down later.**
（如果他的馬沒有不見，他就不會出來找牠，然後他就會待在家裡 ─ 後來房子就塌了下來。）

Unit 6

Unit 7

Unit 8

p.128 1. They lived in a fancy castle hotel.（他們住在一間精美的城堡旅館。）

p.130 2. Food ingredients and daily necessities.（食材和日常用品。）

p.132 3. No, he didn't think so, because he is the member - and he can get a discount.（不，他不這麼認為，因為他是會員——可以打折。）

p.142 1. Rooster.（公雞）

p.144 2. Donkey.（驢子）

p.146 3. They felt so tired.（他們感覺如此疲累。）

p.149 爸：哇靠！你今天真是美到不行！
媽：你這話也說得很美。不過我想看看你今天是哪邊不對勁了！

p.156 1. Because the land was covered with snow.（因為大地被大雪覆蓋了。）

p.158 2. It's beside the valley.（在山谷邊。）

p.160 3. A mountain.（一座山。）

p.163 A: Please tell me if I will become rich in the future?
B: I'm pretty sure... that I'm not able to answer this question.

p.170 1. He felt so hungry and cold.（他很餓且感冒了。）

p.172 2. It's a nice sunny day.（那是個晴朗的好天氣。）

p.174 3. She suggested he should collect some food beforehand.
（她建議他應預先蒐集一些食物。）

p.177 這位生氣的母親過去和他兒子說話：「你最好先洗手」。

Unit 13

p.184   1. He was (as)+ sick as a dog. (他生重病了。)

p.186   2. He checked his blood pressure. (他為他量血壓。)

p.188   3. He ate a rabbit, two frogs, a dozen of eggs, a horse, a boy, a
monkey and an elephant. (他吃了一隻兔子、兩隻青蛙、一打雞蛋、
一頭馬、一個小男孩、一隻猴子和一頭大象。)

p.191   No wonder so many people go to indoor swimming pools. It's
so hot outside.

Unit 14

p.198   1. She wants to become prettier than a swan. (她想變得比天鵝還美。)

p.200   2. There isn't any hot water. (沒有熱水了。)

p.202   3. She thought such a class may be too hard for her.
(她覺得這樣的課程對她來說可能太難了。)

p.205   Looks like it's a bit difficult for them to see who's the better match.

Unit 15

p.212   1. It was held at Disneyland. (在迪士尼樂園舉行)

p.214   2. He wore pajamas. (他穿著睡衣。)

p.216   3. Because there were sleeping pills in his cocktail.
(因為他的雞尾酒裡有安眠藥。)

p.219   is to buy the/some diamonds

227

台灣廣廈 國際出版集團
Taiwan Mansion International Group

國家圖書館出版品預行編目（CIP）資料

我的第一本經典故事親子英文【QR碼行動學習版】/李宗玥、高旭鉥 著；
-- 初版. -- 新北市：國際學村, 2020.09
面；　公分
ISBN 978-986-454-136-2 (平裝附光碟片)
1.英語 2.學習方法 3.親子

805.1　　　　　　　　　　　　　　　　　　109011078

 國際學村

我的第一本經典故事親子英文【QR碼行動學習版】

作　　　者／李宗玥、高旭鉥	編輯中心編輯長／伍峻宏
	編輯／許加慶
	封面設計／林珈伃・內頁排版／菩薩蠻數位文化有限公司
	製版・印刷・裝訂／東豪・鴻源・明和

行企研發中心總監／陳冠蒨	整合行銷組／陳宜鈴
媒體公關組／陳柔彣	綜合業務組／何欣穎

發　行　人／江媛珍
法律顧問／第一國際法律事務所 余淑杏律師・北辰著作權事務所 蕭雄淋律師
出　　版／國際學村
發　　行／台灣廣廈有聲圖書有限公司
　　　　　地址：新北市235中和區中山路二段359巷7號2樓
　　　　　電話：（886）2-2225-5777・傳真：（886）2-2225-8052

代理印務・全球總經銷／知遠文化事業有限公司
　　　　　地址：新北市222深坑區北深路三段155巷25號5樓
　　　　　電話：（886）2-2664-8800・傳真：（886）2-2664-8801
郵政劃撥／劃撥帳號：18836722
　　　　　劃撥戶名：知遠文化事業有限公司（※單次購書金額未達500元，請另付60元郵資。）

■出版日期：2020年09月
ISBN：978-986-454-136-2